It was not unt__ __ __ of Fiammetta, __ __ __ __ __ __ set aside for the royal couple that he allowed himself to think about anything save his duty.

In any detail, that was.

Because he needed to think only of his duty and that had proven surprisingly difficult when Helene—now his *wife*—was around.

He found he was deeply wary of precisely how difficult it had become, even today, when his marriage had always been an inevitability. It had only been a question of *when* and *who* and he had never tried, like some men in his position, to shirk his responsibilities in that area. On the contrary, Gianluca had been attempting to find the perfect queen for his kingdom ever since his father's death some ten years before had catapulted the matter of Gianluca's marriage from a hypothetical *someone*, *someday* to a priority.

But despite his attention to the task, the proper wife—and queen—had remained outside his grasp. Until now.

USA TODAY bestselling, RITA® Award—nominated and critically acclaimed author **Caitlin Crews** has written more than one hundred and thirty books and counting. She has a master's and PhD in English literature, thinks everyone should read more category romance and is always available to discuss her beloved alpha heroes—just ask. She lives in the Pacific Northwest with her comic book—artist husband, is always planning her next trip and will never, ever read all the books in her to-be-read pile. Thank goodness.

Books by Caitlin Crews

Harlequin Presents

Willed to Wed Him
A Secret Heir to Secure His Throne
What Her Sicilian Husband Desires
A Billion-Dollar Heir for Christmas

Innocent Stolen Brides

The Desert King's Kidnapped Virgin
The Spaniard's Last-Minute Wife

The Outrageous Accardi Brothers

The Christmas He Claimed the Secretary
The Accidental Accardi Heir

Visit the Author Profile page
at Harlequin.com for more titles.

Caitlin Crews

WEDDING NIGHT IN
THE KING'S BED

HARLEQUIN
PRESENTS

Recycling programs for this product may not exist in your area.

ISBN-13: 978-1-335-59224-8

Wedding Night in the King's Bed

Harlequin Enterprises ULC
22 Adelaide St. West, 41st Floor
Toronto, Ontario M5H 4E3, Canada
www.Harlequin.com

Printed in U.S.A.

WEDDING NIGHT IN THE KING'S BED

CHAPTER ONE

"You don't have to marry him," Helene Archibald's cousin, best friend, and maid of honor said urgently—and unsolicited—as they stood together in the antechamber of the cathedral.

Outside the small yet ornate little room there were the sounds of organs and a great many people and a grand regal destiny besides, but here there was only the two of them. And Helene's astonishingly prodigious bridal train, pouring all over the old stone floor in a slithering cascade of elegant ivory fabric. Not to mention what had to be every flower in the whole of the Kingdom of Fiammetta, which had been nestled high in the Alps between Italy and France since the Dark Ages, as if to scoff at the frigid January weather with every bright and fragile blossom.

Her cousin, perhaps emboldened by the way her voice echoed between them and the flowers and the dour religious iconography on the stout old walls, carried on with a certain resolute passion. "Who cares if he's a whole king? I'll spirit you away myself."

Helene found this sweet, and unnecessary, but found herself questioning the logistics of the claim all the same. "Would we run off by foot? Down all the closed-off streets monitored by the palace guards and, last I checked, crowded with well-wishers?" She considered, and thinking about an exit strategy she didn't actually want was a nice change from standing about, heart rate alarmingly high, waiting to rush out into the main part of the church so she could then… walk. Very, very slowly up an acre or two of aisle to marry a man who was indeed *a whole king* in front of a crowd both in person and via all the cameras. "And if we somehow made it through, what would we do then? Dressed like this, no less. Would we clamber up the side of the nearest mountain and hope we could slide on our backsides all the way into France?" She gave the endless train a bit of a fluff so that it slithered out even farther across the stones. "In fairness, this might make an excellent slide. Assuming we chose the right mountain, that is. I hear some of these peaks on the Italian side are quite treacherous."

Faith, lovely and loyal Faith, puffed herself up as if prepared to take off in an immediate sprint for the white-capped hills when, until today, Helene could not recall her soft and sweet cousin committing to anything more physically taxing than a saunter down to a sunny beach to lounge about beneath an umbrella. "Only say the word, Helene. I mean it."

"I know you do," Helene assured her. The organ music out in the main part of the cathedral began to climb and swell, soaking in through the walls. There was a sudden uptick in the sounds of muffled coughs and shuffling feet from the hundreds of elite and important guests. She imagined the King himself was already there, standing at the head of the aisle as if the flying buttresses had been arranged to highlight his glory, not God's. They might have been, at that. She smiled, though inside her body, hidden away as it was in yards upon yards of white silk and ivory lace, something darker and deeper... *hummed.* "But I think I might as well go through with it, don't you? Since everyone has gone to all this bother?"

"I hope that is one of your charmless jokes, Helene," said her father, then, closing the door to the rest of the cathedral that she hadn't heard him open. With his usual fastidious precision. Then he merely stood there, pinning her with that cold glare of his. "Of course you're *going through with it*. This is your wedding to the

King of Fiammetta, for the love of all that is holy. It does not require *thought*."

What Helene wanted to say was, *Not for you, Papa, I know.*

But she had long since decided that there was no point arguing with her father. Herbert Marcel Archibald was slim like a wire, always vibrating with outrage and insult. There was nothing fruitful to be gained in debating him on any topic. The last time she had attempted it had been before her lovely, happy, bright beacon of a mother had died.

After Mama had gone, there was nothing to argue about. Helene did not expect her father to *see* her, much less *know* her, and he had not pretended to attempt either one. Instead, he had made his expectations for her excessively clear: she was to make a brilliant marriage, as, indeed, her own mother had done with him. Helene was to carry on this tradition of marrying up. She was to excel in all things so she might make herself nothing short of a shiny prize for him to barter away, the better to bolster his own wealth and consequence, as Archibalds had been doing for generations.

Helene had not exactly been thrilled with this fate, having harbored her share of dreams in which she imagined herself, variously, as an astronaut, a judge, and a mermaid. But she'd remembered the stories her graceful, warm mother had told her. Stories of princesses and castles. Fairy tales and happy endings that came from things like arranged marriages—much nicer to contemplate than the age-old games men like her father preferred to play.

She liked to remind herself that she could have rebelled, if she wished. Helene could have turned her back on her father and all his demands, but whenever the urge to do that rose up in her, she reminded herself that Mama never had. That she had stayed with Herbert and despite the obvious chill, had claimed she was happy.

I am safe and cared for, Helene had heard her mother tell Faith's mother, her sister, long ago. *Not all of us are made for passion. Some of us bloom more quietly.*

Helene had decided, then and there, that if she could bloom as her mother had, that would be a life well spent indeed.

And it had certainly been a frosty half a decade since the cold fall day they'd laid her beloved Mama to rest, but Helene liked to remind herself that she'd *chosen* to stay with her father. To submit to his demands and expectations. To do the things she knew her own mother had done, in her time, and how bad could all that cold civility be, really? She'd grown up watching her parents *freeze* at each other, and her mother had called that a kind of blooming.

She'd started to consider herself an icy little rose.

Just say the word, Faith mouthed at her now.

Because *her* parents had married for love. Something they could do, Helene knew, because her own mother—as eldest daughter—had not.

"Come, Helene," Herbert snapped at her, as if the ceremony was something he could do on his own. As if she was keeping him from *his* wedding.

"Yes, Papa," she murmured, as she always did, shooting a smile Faith's way.

And thought about her mother, who would have loved this day no matter how it came about. A cathedral. A kingdom.

An honest-to-God *king*.

Mama would have thought this was nothing short of a festival of blooming.

Helene took her father's impatient arm, and let Faith tuck her away behind the overtly traditional veil no one had asked her if she wanted to wear. Herbert then led her, with all possible ostentation, to the great doors of the cathedral proper, where the King's royal guard stood with expressions of great solemnity.

No one checked in with her. No one asked if *she* was ready.

Helene told herself that was likely because she *exuded* readiness, as was expected.

The guards waited for a signal from the palace aide dressed in finery that managed to look as capable as it did chic, who cocked her head toward what Helene knew by now was an earpiece. The aide spoke softly.

Inside the main part of the cathedral, the organ music swelled anew, into a piece of music that sounded so ornate it made Helene's bones seem to ache inside her skin—or perhaps, she chided herself with a lot less of the drama she knew her father had always disliked in her mother, it was simply a draft from the cold winter's day outside.

But when Helene thought of her mother's most loved stories, the ones she had told time and again that were the most magical of all, she sighed a little. Quietly, there beneath her veil where no one could hear her. And decided to believe it was the music.

The aide pressed a manicured finger to her ear and nodded at the guards, then smiled by rote at Herbert. Over Helene's swaddled form, making it clear that she was the person here with the least significance.

Or, perhaps, she had been identified as the one least likely to complain.

Faith murmured something that sounded like

Ready when you are, which Helene decided to pretend was about the wedding and not escaping it. She waited a breath, then another, and then moved in front of Helene only when Herbert made a huffing sound, accepting the bouquet the palace aide handed her as she slipped in one of the smaller doors to start down the aisle.

The music carried on, a tumbling, soaring symphony that twined with the humming inside of Helene and made every part of her…electric.

Then the great doors were hauled open. The crowd within rose, turned to look at her, and she settled in for a nice long think about…well. Everything that had led her here.

To this cathedral halfway up a mountain in a tiny kingdom that alpine dreams were made of. Where she had lied by omission to her beloved cousin, because she'd allowed Faith to believe that she was being forced into this marriage. It was easier to pretend that she was. Because Helene wasn't sure she had the vocabulary to explain what had happened to her to make her a far more willing participant than Faith was likely to imagine possible…

Besides, it was a very long walk down the cathedral's main aisle. So long that Helene couldn't really make out *which* figure down there at the end was the man who was the real star of this show today. There was a scrum of finery blocking the view and the bishop himself looked resplendent, and yet she somehow doubted that her august groom would *blend*.

Her groom. The King of Fiammetta himself. One Gianluca San Felice, known far and wide for his stern male beauty as much as his forbidding magnetism that should have scared Helene but, instead, had *hummed* deep within her from the start.

It hummed in her now, too, darker and deeper with every step.

He would shortly be her *husband*, and, one day, the father of her children. At least two, she expected, since Gianluca was in possession of a throne. And everyone knew full well that anyone who happened to find themselves on a throne—or even in the vicinity of one, really—generally preferred to have a distinct line of succession put in place behind them to lock the whole enterprise down for generations to come.

Helene preferred to think about blood and lines of succession as if they were somehow unconnected to *people*. And to *her*. Because otherwise there was only that heavy, odd feeling that settled in her as she thought about children. Or, rather, the act of making said children with Gianluca, more an *immensity* than a *man*.

That thing inside her that she thought was him, or his, *hummed* all the more.

Marrying advantageously, and always ambitiously, was the single task of an heiress, her father had told her. Over and over again. Back when she was small he had talked quite openly about the consolidation of hereditary assets—the usual estate or two—and the way in which that could, if done well, create an upgrade in his own, personal status as well as hers. Which ought to have been her primary goal, clearly. Her mother would catch Helene's eye across the long, polished table where children were permitted to appear only if silent, her bright eyes brimming with laughter.

Later, she would curl up with Helene in the nursery and spin out the most fantastic stories about how Helene's marriage would be a wondrous thing, no matter what her silly Papa imagined. That she and her dashing prince would have adventures and slay dragons, dance at marvelous balls, and live a happy and glorious and magical life.

But when it turned out that Helene was going to be first lovely, then objectively pretty, then really quite beautiful, Herbert had gotten greedy. Especially when Helene had turned out to be clever as well, locked away in her exclusive Swiss boarding school where a certain sort of rich man sent his daughter if he wanted to be absolutely certain that she could have no personal life he did not know all about. There was no sneaking out of the Institut. It was a truly lovely prison, set behind high walls and surrounded by guards, where there were never more than ten girls in each year and all of them were earmarked by others for the sort of lives that took place in hushed, elegant castles of one sort or another the world over.

There wasn't much to do but study, take classes, and dream of Prince Charmings they were not allowed to meet without familial oversight.

Helene had always considered herself lucky that her father actually let her finish her education, which was not the case for many of her schoolmates. Plus the extra finishing year that the school was famous for—because, it was whispered, certain monarchs who married for love had made use of the Institut's *finishing* when their scandalously lower-brow queens needed a quick gloss-up.

She'd graduated in full just before her twentieth birthday and had expected her father to put her directly on the auction block—figuratively, she hoped. She had anticipated a heap of tedious social engagements under her father's watchful eye, where she would have to not only be effortlessly charming as was expected from a graduate of the Institut and the Archibald heiress, but suffer her father's commentary on whether or not he thought she'd hit the notes he wished for her to hit.

In truth, she hadn't been sure that she would make it through a week like that, much less the entire summer season her father had been threatening her with when he'd installed her in his summer estate in Provence that year. The men he had in mind for her were all wealthy and titled and Helene and Faith had texted back and forth about them, tracking them all across the internet, and trying their best to turn their evident flaws—from mistresses to gambling to the kind of partying that never ended well and so on—into charming quirks.

Because it was easier to make it all a game. It was almost fun that way.

Or we could run away, Faith would say, as if she had anything to run from herself, with parents who adored and indulged her. *I think I would make a* smashing *artist in some charmingly bohemian city somewhere, living off my wits and my* creative energy.

I believe, Helene would reply, *that you are thinking of Broadway musicals, not reality.*

And while it was true that reality felt a bit heavier on this side of graduation, with actual candidates for her glorious marriage apparently queueing up across Europe, Helene was still resolved to go through with it. Because her father was not a warm man. This she had always known. But if this was the only way she could show her love to him—the only way she knew how to honor her mother now that she was gone and certainly the only way he could receive it, *if* he could receive it at all—she rather thought it was the least she could do.

She, too, could bloom quietly. Safe and cared for, in a very particular way, as she had been all her life. It was only that her mother had managed to make it seem brighter—but then, Helene could do that too. When she was settled in with the man her father chose for her.

But then, one day, the royal messenger had appeared.

In person, before the first party, where Helene had been expected to make her marriageable debut. He had arrived ostentatiously and had proclaimed the good news: Helene had—by what means, he did not specify—managed to secure the notice of the grand and notably great King of Fiammetta himself, who would very much like to meet her.

It had not been an invitation.

My God, girl, Herbert had seethed at her that very evening, beside himself with notions of crowns and consequence run amok. *If you ruin this, I shall never forgive you.*

Helene had not felt there was anything to be won by pointing out that she had not ruined anything yet. That she had been all that was good and obedient, all her life, so much so that Herbert really ought to have been under the impression that she was biddable.

That he was not, she could admit, pleased her. It must mean that her real self lurked *just there* no matter how diffident and obliging she attempted to act in his presence.

Accepting the King's kind invitation that wasn't an invitation at all had been an involved process.

Helene had met with a succession of aides, each of whom had arrived with a new agenda and different versions of combative interview styles wrapped up in deadly courtesy. They had seen her alone and with her father. She had been required to surrender all her devices with a list of all her passwords to anything a person might wish to access online. She had been called upon to account for what seemed like her every last movement since she was a child.

Usually they already knew the answers themselves, but wanted to see what she would say.

You texted your cousin about our last meeting. The most ferociously correct of all the aides had confronted her one day, about a month into the process. *You told her, if I recall it correctly, that you were beginning to suspect that the King might not, in fact, exist. Is that not so?*

I did text that, Helene had agreed, and had been glad her father was not present. He would not have liked the appalled way the woman had gazed at her. He would have forbidden her from contacting Faith, possibly ever again, given he had never cared much for Helene's mother's family anyway. Helene had laughed without meaning to. *But can you blame me?*

The King himself had descended the next day.

She almost tripped, here in the cathedral, as she recalled it. She wasn't sure how she kept from sprawling out in an inelegant heap right there with the eyes of the Kingdom upon her—though perhaps her father's grip on her had something to do with it.

Helene let him guide her along. And let herself think back to that June morning that still stood out so clearly to her, marking a *before* and an *after*.

Kings did not simply *turn up* in places, not even when they were attempting to go incognito. So while it was true that he had *descended* upon her father's tidy château, there had been some small bit of notice. Another messenger had appeared that morning, followed swiftly by an advance team who had treated her father's estate to a sweeping security review even though several other similar reviews had already been undertaken.

While the King's security secured the perimeter of the property, again, Herbert had leaped at the chance to direct Helene in how she needed to behave on such a momentous occasion. He had conferred with both the palace aides and his own staff to curate the perfect introductory scene.

No detail was beneath his notice.

He sent Helene back to her rooms three different times because he felt her hair was first inappropriate, then wanton, and then again, too casual. He was only satisfied when her long, usually wavy, dark brown hair was tamed into submission and woven into a loose French braid that he deemed neither too casual nor too sophisticated, both *kisses of death*.

Her outfit was subjected to the same scrutiny. And if Helene had learned anything in her time at the Institut, it was not to ask perfectly reasonable questions of unreasonable people. Like, for example, shouldn't she simply present *herself* to the King? Given that it was she who had caught his notice? It was certainly not down to her father's machinations—Herbert had never dared imagine *royalty* might be within his reach.

Ladies, she had been taught again and again,

did not lower themselves to argue. They endured with dignity and then, when it was time, they *encouraged* their way toward different outcomes.

Meaning, she bit her tongue. She changed as directed into these trousers and then that gown. She exchanged bold accessories for subtle hints. She scrubbed off this round of cosmetics and started anew, time and again, until her father deemed what she wore suitable enough.

How funny, Helene thought now as she measured one step, then the next, that she couldn't remember any longer what that final outfit had been. Every time she thought she'd come round to the final choice, she remembered instead that her father had ordered her to change it. Or that one of the palace aides had lifted a brow at the sight of it, which her father had taken to mean regal disdain from afar.

What she remembered distinctly was that she had never felt less like herself when she'd been ordered, at last, to go and wait in one of the drawing rooms where she was directed to arrange herself artfully on the settee. Her father would greet His Majesty, she was informed, and then they would all sit down for a bit of a chat. Perhaps there would be a drink, depending on what sort of man this king was, and then Herbert would excuse himself.

And I trust that you will behave as you ought, her father had barked at her, right there in front of the King's advance team and the entirety of his own household staff. *When in doubt, smile and remain silent.*

She'd sat in the chosen drawing room, practicing. She and the other girls in her year at the Institut had actually held a contest to see who had the most *enigmatic smile* of the lot, because they all knew full well that the right one could be used as a weapon. Sadly, Helene had never mastered the art. There was too much hope and too many fairy tales in her smile.

In that she was her mother's daughter.

And she'd grown rather cross with herself as she waited, because she was actually getting nervous. Helene had not understood why *she* should be nervous about some man she didn't even know and might very well never lay eyes upon again. It didn't matter if he was a king or one of her father's business associates. It was all the same to her, wasn't it.

What she chose to believe, then and always, was that her real job was to make certain that she followed her mother's directives as best she could. Meaning that no matter the situation, she was to look for the magic. She was to find the marvel in the thing, and no matter if it was decidedly un-marvelous.

And if there are no Prince Charmings to be found? she'd asked, presciently, she thought. *What will I do then?*

You'll look deep and you'll find him, her sweet mother had replied, squeezing her hand tight. *I have no doubt,* mon chou.

Nervousness didn't help anything, she decided then, and she'd gotten up from her decorative position on the settee her father had indicated. She'd moved over to the great doors, done in a mullioned glass that opened up over one of the château's many patios. This one in particular let out to her mother's garden.

That was not why her father had chosen it, Helene knew. He had chosen it because all of the art on the walls were recognizable masterpieces. Herbert did like to show off.

Helene had opened up the doors and stepped outside, breathing in the sweet summer air. She'd walked over to the edge of the patio, glanced back over her shoulder, and had decided she had plenty of time to pad down the stairs, breathe deep of her mother's favorite flowers, and collect herself.

Blooming lavender made her feel safe again. Hints of rosemary made her smile. And the first flush of the summer roses felt like the sort of happy-ever-afters her mother had always loved best.

Helene had breathed deep.

And when she turned around again, prepared to start back in and arrange herself artfully, silently, and dutifully once more, he was there.

She had squatted down to get a really deep breath—or ten—of her favorite fragrance, a mixture of all those hints of herbs and flowers that reminded her so strongly of her mother, and so he had seemed tall enough to block out the sky itself. Helene had stopped breathing. Her throat had gone almost painfully dry. At the same time, there was a sudden deep and thudding thing that nearly knocked her back on her behind into the dirt—

And it took her far too long to understand it was her own heart.

She gazed up at him, all the way up at him, and deep inside her—low and insistent—that humming thing took root.

He made her shake from the inside out.

She did not ask it was really him. She knew him at once, without question. She had seen the photographs of him that his own staff had presented her, and the many pictures of him that littered the internet, but Helene knew she would have recognized him all the same.

Because he stood there at the top of the patio stairs as if he expected nothing else than to find women—if not everyone, everywhere—writhing about in the dirt at his feet.

As if they often did exactly that.

Helene knew full well that they did. She'd seen the pictures. He was, according to many sources, the most eligible man in the world.

And for a moment there, she couldn't decide if she ought to throw herself face down on the dirt before him or not, because every lesson she had ever learned about comportment and elegant manners at the Institut seemed to have deserted her entirely.

There was nothing of *her* left. There was only that humming. There was only him, the actual king, and somehow, one single stray thought: that this man was not the least bit photogenic.

He was widely held to be handsome. She'd thought so herself when she'd studied the many pictures of him and had even harbored a thought or two—that she would deny if asked, because it seemed silly and unseemly at once—that perhaps this whole arranged marriage deal might not be as terrible as she'd imagined because of this handsomeness.

Perhaps he would be wretched, she'd told herself, but at least he would be pleasant to look at. For Helene was astonished to discover that, if anything, every photograph she'd ever seen of

Gianluca San Felice, King of Fiammetta, made him look ugly.

That was the effect of his stark, stern, overwhelming male beauty. It was so much *more* in person. It was like a force field.

He struck her like a natural disaster. A storm of epic proportions.

That was the sort of *beautiful* this man was.

Helene was not certain how she withstood the first sight of him. She had stood up, somehow, though her body had not felt like her own. She'd felt sunburned, suddenly, as if she'd been out in the summer sun for hours instead of mere moments. As if it had roasted her very bones.

The cold, German-accented voice of the Institut headmistress made itself known inside her then, counting out seconds like a metronome. And she remembered, almost too late, to drop into the appropriate curtsy one typically offered at the sight of royalty.

Helene was grateful, in a way she never had been before, for the headmistress's insistence that they practice these things again and again and again. She was grateful that her body did what it had practiced so many times with ease, as if it was all muscle memory, because it gave her time to figure out how to breathe again. How to keep herself from toppling over. How to try her best to wrestle with that bizarre sunburn that seemed as prickly and hot on the inside as it was on her skin.

"Rise," the King ordered her softly enough, but with evident command, and she did.

And then, for an endless, airless moment, he simply studied her.

That prickling sensation got worse. Or better, maybe. In any case, it was more and it washed over her, changing her as it went. Shifting things she hadn't known were there, or moveable. There were too many competing urges inside her, then. She'd wanted to say something smart to impress him. She'd wanted to prove, with a few carefully chosen words, that she was so much more than whatever he'd seen in whatever dossier he'd received on her. That she wasn't her father, who she understood was not a man that other men admired.

She was *this close* to announcing to this impossibly compelling man, this *king*, that she was a whole person, brimming with contradictions and obsessions and marvelous, secret bits that she hardly knew herself.

But she didn't dare.

In a few moments I am going to go around to the front of this château and make my official entrance, he told her. Eventually. He did not smile, but she felt the urge to smile back at him as if he had. *But you see, I have learned that it behooves me to take a sneak peek first at whatever woman I am set to meet.*

She started to speak, then remembered that he was no ordinary man. He was a king and there was etiquette for all interactions between kings and commoners, and for all she knew this was a trap.

But his eyes were so dark, like the middle of the longest night, and they gleamed. *You may speak freely. After all, I am the one lurking about in your garden, am I not?*

She knew better than to take him at his word. Not entirely. This was a game, and obviously one he had played before. But she did not remain silent, either. *What is it you're hoping to find?* she asked. *When you take these sneak peeks of yours?*

It is hugely instructive, he replied, easily enough that she realized, with a certain dizzy sensation, that he could be charming. This immensity of a man who stood before her so easily, so used was he to being gazed up at in this manner. *Often the house is in disarray, or too clean, like a crime scene of some kind. Often the woman I am to meet is barking unhinged orders at servants, screaming at everyone she sees, and otherwise behaving in a manner she would not if she knew I was watching.*

Forgive me, Helene had said. *But I am given*

*to understand that a great many royal person-
ages often behave in precisely this manner.*

It had been a risky gambit. She'd waited for
him to draw himself up in umbrage and affront,
and march away, having crossed her off his list.
And she'd wondered what had possessed her
when it surely would have been easier to simply
murmur something inoffensive instead.

Perhaps she had even been holding her breath.

Though she forgot about that—and everything else—when he smiled.

If his gaze was night, his smile was a whole,
bright summer, and as he beamed it down at
her she saw entirely too much. That he was a
man, a mortal, and more—that he could indeed
make a woman a fine husband, if he chose. And
then, in a rush of heat and wonder and something sharp, like need, she saw the kind of future she hadn't dared imagine for herself unfurl
before her. A hand to hold quietly, in the back
of a car, no words required. Dancing with her
head tipped back and his smile all the music
she needed. Laughter, and children, and rooms
they made sing with the force of all the things
they were to each other—

All of that as he gazed down at her, that smile
such a bit of unexpected magic that she rather
thought the deep black night of his eyes was
shot through with stars.

A great many royal personages are appalling human beings, he'd said, the smile in his voice now too, like dawn breaking over a new day, all of it laced with the very things she'd just seen stampede through her. *Why do you imagine I have come to look for this behavior in advance? I know it too well and wish to avoid it, at all costs.*

I'm sorry to disappoint you, she replied, and her smile felt reckless. But it was impossible to contain. *I suppose I could soundly abuse the plants, if I liked, but I doubt if I did that they would bloom as they do. This was my mother's garden and I tended it with her when I was small. The fragrance of the things she planted makes me happy. That's all.*

His smile faded, but what took its place was more complicated. More…considering. *And this is what you wished? To be happy, today of all days?*

This is what I wish every day, Helene corrected him, still smiling, though she dropped her gaze to the shoots of lavender and ran her fingertips down the buds. *It is not always achievable, I grant you.*

It occurred to her that could be taken as a slight, but he'd still been looking at her in that narrow manner, as if she was a calculation he needed to solve. *And if I told you that I do not believe in happiness?* His tone was light.

We must all believe in something, Your Majesty. Surely.

I believe in duty, Miss Archibald.

My mother used to say that we must plant flowers wherever we can make them grow, instead of waiting for flowers to bloom. Duty is what you make of it, in other words.

He'd studied her for another moment, and she had never felt anything like the weight of his gaze. The intensity of his attention. The heat of him, like his very own sun.

That prickling within her seemed to melt into the humming until it was all one thing, shivering and hot, a beautiful tornado. It tore through her, laying waste to whoever she'd been before, so sudden and so devastating that she wasn't sure if she'd drawn a single breath since the moment she'd looked up and seen him there.

King Gianluca inclined his head, and some odd sort of light or other gleamed then, in the encompassing darkness of his gaze.

I look forward to meeting you, Miss Archibald, he said in his commanding way, and then he turned and strode back around the side of the house. Taking the air and the blue sky and the gold and purple of Provence with him.

For a moment she'd stood there, dazed. She wasn't sure if she'd imagined the whole thing— but then her body was moving of its own accord again. It carried her back up the stairs, into through the same mullioned glass doors to settle herself on that delicate settee as if she was still the same person she'd been before she'd gone out into the garden.

As if she could ever be the same again, seared straight through as she was.

It had seemed a lifetime, though she supposed it could as easily have been mere moments, before her father's voice could be heard in the hall outside. Before the palace aides found their way inside, and then, with great fanfare, announced His Royal Majesty, King Gianluca of Fiammetta himself.

Helene rose, then sank into the curtsy that was expected of her—no matter that she had already performed this mark of respect outside, he had acted as if that meeting was to be kept between them, surely—and when she rose, he was smiling directly at her once again.

Not the same smile. This one was a slight curve of his hard, stern lips and no more, but Helene had known all the same. She had known, at that very moment, that she was going to marry him. That she would marry him and that whole future she could see sweeping out before her would be hers.

It was sweeping through her now, here in the cathedral at last. It had carried her along through the rest of the summer, walks in that garden and visits in her father's parlors, that smile of his so rare and unpredictable and yet world-changing every time. It had buoyed her during her father's lectures and critiques that grew more scathing in the lead-up to the actual proposal, such as it was, involving as it did meetings with her father and staff and stacks of contracts to sign and too much attention given to the few words he said to her personally, where everyone else could hear, that smile she'd come to think of as hers turned to stars in his gaze.

Stars and a smile, that was what she'd held on to that fall, as her life turned inside out and she became the property of the palace, trotted out for photo opportunities at events both grand and humble. The King's date for another royal's wedding abroad. Or a seemingly casual walk together on a crisp afternoon in Fiammetta, caught by engineered "happenstance" and plastered across every gossip rag in existence.

They had never been truly alone, and so she'd taken that smile and their imagined future and the stars in his dark night gaze with her to bed, curled around them like pillows she could shape to hold her as she wished, and dreamed about what was to come.

And when she lifted her gaze toward the end

of the aisle once more, she found him standing there at last.

Resplendent and self-possessed, and even more shockingly magnetic than she'd remembered, when she'd last seen him the night before during a highly photographed celebratory dinner.

His dark black gaze seemed to hold fast on her as she moved down the aisle and as it did, it kicked off a new lightning storm within her even as it settled her, somehow, in the same breath.

There had to be another mile to walk, at the least, but Helene scarcely noticed.

All she could feel was him. That gaze. That storm inside her. She trembled, and knew her father felt it where their arms were linked because the crook of his elbow tightened around her hand, and the look he shot at her was more of a shout.

It confused her for a moment. But then she realized. Herbert thought she was having second thoughts.

When nothing could be further from the truth.

Because this was the secret she hadn't told even Faith. That there wasn't a single part of her, inside or out, that did not wish to marry this man. And he could have been anyone. It had nothing to do with kings or crowns, thrones or settlements. She didn't care about any of that.

She would have married Gianluca San Felice no matter who he was.

Because when he looked at her, her entire body blazed into life. When he took her hand in his, she felt thick and wet between her legs, and silly straight through. He made her breasts ache. He made her want to press herself against him, again and again, and try out the things she'd only read in books.

Her cousin might not have approved of this marriage, but Helene had known that it was what she wanted back on the first day she'd met Gianluca. It felt like an inevitability, something necessary—not a choice. A lightning bolt from above and she had no choice but to meet it head-on or let it burn her to ash.

Though this felt a lot like both.

After an eternity, her father delivered her to the head of the aisle, passing off his daughter to this king who claimed her.

Gianluca took her hand and everything in her ignited, the way it always did. That hum became a roar, and wound itself into a delirious tangle everywhere it touched.

And then everything became that tangle. That rush of heat and wonder.

That glorious future dancing before her, stars

and his smile, the things that would be only theirs when they were finally alone together.

That humming within her only expanded as the ceremony began, until it was her turn to speak and she could not simply shout out her joy at this union the way she wanted to do. She had to sound elegant enough for a king. Sophisticated enough to become his queen.

She repeated what the bishop said, and then, finally, it was time. Gianluca slid a ring on her finger to match the diamond solitaire he'd put there a few months before. His mouth so stern, his dark eyes so deep.

And there were only two words to say, but Helene meant them with every part of her aching, needy body, and the whole of her soul.

"I do," she whispered.

Then he lifted the veil and kissed her for the very first time, making her his wife.

And teaching her how precious little she knew about fire.

CHAPTER TWO

IT WAS NOT until Gianluca, the King of Fiammetta whether he liked it or not, sat at the high table set aside for the royal couple's use while the spectacularly elegant reception went on all around him, that he allowed himself to think about anything save his duty.

In any detail, that was.

Because he needed to think only of his duty and that had proven surprisingly difficult when Helene—now his *wife*—was around.

He found he was deeply wary of precisely how difficult it had become, even today, when his marriage had always been an inevitability. It had only been a question of *when* and *who* and he had never tried, like some men in his position, to shirk his responsibilities in that area. On the contrary, Gianluca had been attempting to find the perfect queen for his kingdom ever since his father's death some ten years before had catapulted the matter of Gianluca's marriage from a hypothetical *someone, someday* to a priority.

But despite his attention to the task, the proper wife—and queen—had remained outside his grasp. Until now.

Until Helene, who was not afraid of the dirt or of saying things to him others would not dare. Until Helene, who had a certain earthy appeal that had him very nearly ready to toss this whole party out the front doors of the palace so he could explore it all he liked—

Yet that was one of the details he was *not* going to think about. Not quite yet.

Because unlike his parents, he had taken his time seeking out the right woman for the job— and he had no illusions on that score. He might flatter himself that being his wife might be a position any woman would aspire to, but being Queen of Fiammetta was a job. A thankless career, in many ways, with no promotions and no deviations, though there were a few perks along the way. He needed to make certain that he knew what he was getting into with any woman put forward for the position. He had studied the hopefuls who had been trotted out for his approval and he had only made this choice after digging, deep, into all there was to know about Helene Archibald—now Her Majesty the Queen of Fiammetta, for good or ill.

She was out there in the sea of people before him, talking with that cousin of hers while all the self-important people in his kingdom studied her, looking for flaws—when there were none. Helene was as poised as she was beautiful, gracious to all who came to bestow their well wishes upon her even when it was clear that they were poking around for gossip fodder, and kept sliding looks in his direction.

Always fully cognizant of precisely where he was in the ballroom at any given time.

He was inclined to think this marriage might be more than good. It might just be the best decision he'd made yet.

But he did not gaze at her the way he wished to do. Because he did not intend to make his marriage the talking point of his reign, as his father had done, not even tonight. He would not allow it.

Gianluca had long practice in hiding his true thoughts behind a neutral expression, and he was glad of it now. Because he didn't like to think about his parents too much. Not if it could be avoided. There were the darker, private moments he had half convinced himself were merely nightmares he'd had as a child—but he did not permit himself to dig into *that*. What he did not care for, and what offended him still, was the stain that their overly publicized antics had left on this kingdom. And because of that stain, the weight he felt upon him at all times to prove himself nothing like the pair of them.

He would never allow any queen of his to behave as his own mother had, making a mockery of her vows and dragging the crown through the mud. Parading the private business of the palace out into the public eye and making certain it stayed there in some twisted, misguided bid for revenge because—as far as Gianluca could discern—her *feelings had been hurt.*

And if the feelings he recalled most vividly from his childhood had been vile and unsettling, alarming and often frightening—

But no. That was a story his mother told, when surely, if it had been as bad as all that, she would not have stayed. The truth, then and now, was that she was addicted to the drama. And the attention she could wring from it all.

He checked himself then because too many eyes were upon him now, as always. He inclined his head toward a pack of diplomats. He gave his public version of a smile to a set of his distant cousins. But he did not beckon anyone to approach him and thus no one dared.

Not even the loathsome Lady Anselma, one of his mother's boon companions, who had made herself a tidy little cottage industry over the years as his mother's "unnamed source from within the palace." He smiled, as he knew he must, but Gianluca had no use for her or the rest of the many Dowager Queen Elettra apologists in the Kingdom, forever making up excuses for his mother's actions and trying them out one after the next when the previous one failed to garner enough sympathy. As it always did, eventually.

He knew all the excuses by heart. They claimed she had been too young when she'd married King Alvize a few months shy of her nineteenth birthday, when Gianluca had already been in the military at the same age—an adult in every sense of the term and expected to act accordingly. Elettra had been an adult who had been perfectly capable of competing in her beloved dressage circles at the highest levels. *The Champion Queen*, they had called her when she'd won the highest medal in the sport six months before she'd been elevated to the Fiammettan throne.

No one had ever suggested she was too young or too foolish to compete at that level.

They claimed she hadn't known any better, which Gianluca had never understood. For it was made perfectly clear in the wedding vows themselves. Were her supporters truly claiming that an aristocratic young champion gold medalist…could not comprehend a set of wedding vows? One either followed them or did not, but they were not *confusing*.

Surely his mother's behavior made her character plain.

It always had for him.

His favorite—which was to say, the least persuasive argument, to his mind—was that his own father was to blame for the betrayals that had been practiced upon him. Sometimes he remembered those stormy nights inside the King and Queen's apartments, when he'd hid from the shouting—but he knew, now, that his father's reactions had been warranted. Because there were always the endless stories of his father's first great love, the Lady Lorenza, who had been promised to another and raised by a man who kept *his* vows to his daughter's betrothed. No matter that Lorenza had dallied with the King before her official engagement.

Not to mention, it was accepted fact that Alvize and Lorenza had consummated their feelings in a scorching affair that had rendered the tabloids breathless with speculation that Alvize might reverse centuries of Fiammettan tradition by marrying her.

When everyone knew that it was written in the law of the Kingdom that the King must marry a virgin bride.

His mother was the one who had accused his

father for the sake of that drama she craved, he thought now, firmly, as he always did. When she was the one who had sinned.

Gianluca had no sympathy for anyone involved. His mother had been a disaster but his father had been the King and should have handled her better, he thought now, gazing out at the many luminaries who graced the great hall of the palace tonight. Lady Lorenza and his mother were among them, of course, because *he* upheld the traditions and expectations and customs of his position. No matter what.

He could not help but reflect, as he had many times before, that his father had known perfectly well what the rules were. They had been made abundantly clear to Alvize in the same way they had been imparted upon Gianluca when he was still a small child. The many palace tutors whose job it was to see to it that the young kings knew their own traditions made certain of it.

What Gianluca could not get past was one simple truth: if his father had intended to marry the woman he seemingly loved so deeply, then he should not have let himself get so carried away with her. Even if the so-called scorching affair had been perfectly innocent in private, which Gianluca doubted, his father should have made certain the tabloids never got wind of his attachment to the Lady Lorenza in the first place. If he had been swept away by her, as everyone seemed to think, he should have dedicated himself to negotiations with not only his beloved's father, but the match she'd been meant to make all along.

That he had not done so, to Gianluca's mind, meant that he had not been quite as madly in love as everyone liked to pretend. While either excusing him or demonizing him.

And yet he had knowingly walked wide-eyed into his own destruction, because he'd chosen a woman like Elettra, who craved attention above all things. She could have been in no doubt that Alvize's affections were engaged elsewhere, though she still claimed she had not known of the King's very famous love affair until after the wedding. And it did not matter to Elettra that the object of her husband's supposed affections was married to another by then, and was, by all accounts, faithful to him.

What mattered to Elettra was that *she* was not the center of the King's attention, then or ever, and so she had acted out.

Again and again and again.

She had made no secret of her affairs. She'd thrown them not only in her husband's face, but had made sure that her exploits were tabloid fodder at all times. She sent out her minions to keep her name forever in the press, forever stoking that same fire, forever embarrassing the palace, forever carrying on in full view of all of Europe and the whole of the world besides.

Elettra thought she was thereby punishing the King.

And Gianluca could not say whether that had worked, because his father's emotions had always been hidden in public, but volatile in the palace. And this particular topic had been one his father had declared off-limits when Gianluca had still been an adolescent—unless Alvize was the one raging about it.

The people, meanwhile, had chosen sides in the streets and otherwise told poll after poll that they would prefer a lot less of a soap opera from their monarchy.

What Gianluca did know, however, was that he was the one who had to clean up the mess they'd left behind after his father's death. His parents' scandals were now his problem. Not that he could recall his father, in the whole of his lifetime, ever indicating that he was aware his only son and heir would be left to handle the fallout of the soap opera he'd let play on.

His mother, on the other hand, knew all too well. She was here tonight on sufferance.

Yet Gianluca was not particularly surprised that his mother had somehow failed to get the

message he knew full well must have been delivered to her by every aide in the palace and
half of the royal guard. Because there was a
ripple in the crowd below the raised dais where
he sat and there she was. As perhaps he should
have expected. Marching right up to him as if
she had that right. As if he did not normally
make certain she was kept from his sight.

But then, Elettra knew that he would not behave with anything but the utmost courtesy in
front of all these people and his proper new
bride. She was counting on it.

Gianluca disliked that she was right.

"Will you not rise to greet your own mother?"
she asked with a merry sort of laugh that they
both knew would look like a bit of maternal de-
votion, as if the two of them were close. "On
your wedding day?"

"Your invitation was all the greeting I intend
to give, Madam," he replied icily, though he had
to keep the affront from his expression as she
helped herself to the chair reserved for his new
bride and sat in it. With, again, a familiarity
that they both knew would send any number of
false messages to the avidly watching throng.

This was another reason Gianluca did not
trust her. She was much too good at these games
while his father had too often seemed a victim
to his own temper.

"The new queen seems like a lovely girl," Elettra said quietly. "But does she know, truly, what she is in for with you? This heart of stone you carry in your chest might crush you both. Not to mention your unwillingness to forgive. You cannot think these will serve you well now you are wed."

"Have you come to give me marital advice?"

She had the grace to wince, however faintly. "I do not offer advice, Gianluca. How could I? Still, you might learn from my example."

"But here's the difference, Madam," Gianluca said, leaning closer to her with a faint smile that would be read as possibly affectionate from afar. He hoped. No doubt reading the truth of his feelings, his personal aide started forward, but Gianluca stopped the man with the barest shake of his head. "My bride will not betray me. She is not you."

And he was well used to his mother's performances by now. The way she tipped her head back as if struck. The way she let her shoulders sag, making herself the very picture of despair for one, single beat before rallying again... But then, she had always been an accomplished actress. And he knew full well he was not the audience to whom she played.

She liked a crowd, did Elettra.

"My bride does not require your concern,

Madam," he said, and rose then, ending the conversation before Elettra could up the ante. "You and she will have no relationship. I see no reason to let you poison the well, simply because you find yourself bored once again."

"I haven't even met the girl," his mother protested.

Gianluca inclined his head with his polished smile on display for all to see. "By design."

He left her there at the table, making his way through his own ballroom and nodding to all those who bowed before him as he passed—taking care to look like the merry groom he rather thought he actually was, all things considered.

Not that he had much experience with merriment.

He blamed his parents for that, too. And try though he did to put Elettra from his mind, he could not understand why his mother still, after all these years, pretended she did not understand how things were done. Or that he was not going to indulge her displays like his father had—something she should have picked up a long while ago, because he had not exactly hidden his criticisms of her even before his father's death. What she should have done tonight was express her gratitude that he had allowed her to attend this wedding at all.

Instead she spoke of his *stone heart*. As if,

were that the case, she had not rolled that boulder there herself.

But he caught sight of Helene and thrust all thoughts of the Dowager Queen aside. He made his way toward his bride, who was now in the clutches of her own questionable father, as the grasping little man steered her around the room like a prize bit of horseflesh that he intended to use to open as many doors as he could.

For some men's ambition only grew through their children.

Gianluca knew a lot about that, too.

A hush fell over the little group as he approached, though he noted that it was Helene's father who was the last to take note that the King himself had appeared.

"If I may claim my queen," Gianluca said, quietly enough. But when he spoke, his words created a kind of ripple of reaction. As if he had shouted when he had not. He was used to this effect, so he used it to take Helene's hand and draw her to him.

And he liked very much the way she came to him, that smile all over her face and her steps so light, her lovely eyes fixed to his.

Gianluca was not his father. He was not in love with another woman. He was not in love at all, of course—though he did not mind if the watching crowd thought otherwise. Or even if

Helene did, as a sheltered girl likely might in her situation. He had found himself averse to the very notion of love from a young age, so often did his parents bandy it about the palace, hurling it at each other as if the word itself was a weapon.

At the same time, he could not deny that he had liked Helene from the start.

All the options that had been presented to him over the past ten years had been beautiful. He supposed that was a prerequisite when a man was a king. But he had found that most of the beautiful women offered to him were the same sort of beautiful that had nothing to do with their specific looks. They had all been cold. Icy, even. They would, each and every one of them, have looked lovely at his side. They would all have complemented him in their own ways and he imagined that would have been pleasing enough.

But Helene made him...hungry.

He took her hand now, aware that it was cool to the touch but then heated, quickly. He could see that same fire in her cheeks, and watched, fascinated, as it turned the skin of her neck a faint peach hue.

And he remembered standing outside on a summer's morning in France, catching sight of her for the first time. The way she gazed up at him from where she crouched down with surprising elegance to stroke a sprig of lavender in a simple shift dress that only drew attention to her lush beauty.

She had looked at him with a kind of stunned longing, as if he was a wish fulfilled.

When she could not possibly have expected him to appear as he had. They never did. Most of them had never seen him at all before they were formally introduced and never knew that he had seen them first, unguarded.

Helene was no ice queen, no cardboard cutout. She was not yet another exquisitely blueblooded heiress whose looks vaguely resembled that of an Afghan hound no matter what her coloring might have been. Her father had all the charisma of a pillar of salt, but Helene herself had been something of a revelation.

What shocked him was that, all these months later, she still was.

Her mouth was wide and generous and if she were the sort of woman to paint her lips crimson and wear a dress that made love to her curves, he had no doubt that she could bring whole populations of men to their knees. That she *could*, but did not, only added to her mystique.

Helene's eyes were wide and large and a deep, velvety shade of brown ringed in gold. Her hair was thick and dark and waved languorously down her back tonight, half of it twisted into something breathtakingly elegant at the back of her head to better accentuate the tiara he had presented her from the family collection.

Gianluca had not known until he'd seen her in that garden, all curves and that mouth, how deeply he had longed, the whole of his life, to get his hands on a figure like hers.

It made everything feel…fraught.

He had always thought of his wedding night as one more simple expression of his duty to the crown. Gianluca had always hoped to find a suitable bride with whom that duty would not be a chore, but that was as far as his thinking on the matter had ever gone. Mostly he had been focused on making sure any queen of his had not only a spotless reputation, but was self-possessed enough that he need not fear she would follow in his mother's footsteps.

And yet tonight, he found that all he could think about when he let himself consider the fact of his marriage was the marital bed.

It was unseemly.

He knew too well where *feelings* led.

But no matter what might have surged about within him, Gianluca was a king, not some callow youth, so he pulled her into his arms as the party arranged itself around them to create space on the dance floor.

The orchestra immediately shifted to accommodate him, as was only right and proper, but Gianluca lost all interest in what was going on around them. Because she was his wife. His queen. And she was lush and she was curvy, and yet she was as light in his arms as if she had trained in ballet all these years when he knew full well she had not.

"Are you enjoying the party?" he asked, as if he was a lesser man with no conversational skills whatever.

And he watched, captivated despite himself, as her eyes lit up with laughter. All she did was incline her head, ever so slightly. "I can hardly say that I don't like it, can I?" That gleam seemed to intensify, as if it was inside him, too. "It would be churlish. After all, this is meant to be my party as well, isn't it?"

Gianluca had wanted to *like* his wife. He had not planned to find her *quite* so fascinating. It was making it difficult to be kind, but distant, as intended.

Because he would not litter his rule with the personal explosions that had so marked his father's.

"You can feel anything you like," he said, with perhaps more severity than necessary when they were waltzing about the royal ballroom. On their wedding night.

But she did not react the way another woman might have. He had the sense of her laughter all around him, yet the only place it appeared was her gaze. "As long as I am not so ill-mannered as to say it out loud, which, of course, no daughter of my father would ever dream of doing. I understand, Your Majesty."

"We are married now, Helene." He was not sure he could remember if he'd actually tasted her name on his mouth before. Had he? Certainly not when she was his. He found himself pulling her closer than was strictly encouraged, if one's manners were as scrupulous and above reproach as his had always been before now. "Surely you can call me by my name. When we are alone."

Another wave of laughter, yet she did not laugh. But the gold in her eyes seemed to get brighter by the moment. "Does this count as alone? Here in the middle of the crowded ballroom?" But then she smiled as she relented. *"Gianluca."*

And it took Gianluca a few moments to realize that what moved in him then was pure satisfaction. For what else could it be, this stampeding glory of a feeling that washed through him, head to toe?

He had done it.

Despite everything, he had made certain that

the sins of his parents would stop with them. He had drawn a line under their nonsense at last—and there was no point dragging old nightmares into the light. No questioning if it was really nonsense, not all these years after his father's death. It was easier to think of the soap opera aspect and make sure he did not succumb to such behavior himself. And it was not that he had doubted that he would succeed, because of course he'd expected he would. Nonetheless, that this particular task had been dealt with at last pleased him.

That she was such a delight pleased him more.

And it was also possible that simply holding this new queen in his arms pleased him most of all—because he had succeeded, he assured himself. That was the only thing that mattered to him.

He had spent a series of not unpleasant hours with her in Provence, watched from varying distances by his people and hers, and they had talked of all the things strangers talk about—weather and small things, anecdotes and reminiscences, all in service of taking the measure of each other.

It had been far more entertaining than he'd expected.

Once he'd proposed, naturally, there had been little time or need for private moments. The presentation of a potential new queen to his people had required a focused strategy, the better to get the sort of photo opportunities that would allow every citizen of his kingdom to feel as if they knew Helene in the short few months they had to get used to her.

Gianluca knew that it was the fashion these days for royal men such as himself to date out in the open whenever possible, thus allowing the public to speculate about the worthiness of each and every woman seen on his arm. And then to offer unsolicited opinions about whether or not the woman in question was prepared to take on the job, as if he was not perfectly capable of judging such things himself.

But Gianluca was not modern. Not like that. The old ways were what had kept his family on the throne of Fiammetta for many centuries. What was good enough for the first of his name was good enough for him, as he always liked to say. He would have had the words tattooed into his skin, but that felt redundant. Those words were who he was.

His grandparents had gotten to know each other when they were already married, and really only once they had a baby on the way. If then. Gianluca smiled at the thought, because he could hear the way his grandmother would have said the words herself. She had never been one for too much *mawkish intimacy*, as she would have called it. She had famously preferred distance and her own company. And given that she and his grandfather had ruled the nation through turmoil aplenty for some fifty years, none of it emanating from their marriage, how could Gianluca not look to them as his guides?

But as he gazed around the ballroom, pleased that he had crossed this particular thorny issue off of his list, his eyes caught on the one person at the party who seemed to have no issue whatsoever scowling.

Directly at him, the King of Fiammetta, when no one else would dare.

"Is your cousin well?" he asked his bride.

This time, her laugh was audible. "Faith is perfectly well. Just rather...protective."

"Do you require protection?" he asked, and there was something, then, in the space between them. He could not say he knew what it was. He could not say he liked it.

It had something to do with her small, elegant hand in his, skin to skin. It was the memory of standing at the altar and peeling back her veil, then pressing his mouth to hers for the very first time.

That moment poked at him, and Gianluca didn't like that, either. He had congratulated himself at length on not touching her at all in the lead-up to their wedding. It was a long road between untouched and no longer a virgin, of course, but he had not taken so much as a step along it.

He had been certain that he had made that choice simply because it was the right one. He had felt morally superior.

Then he had kissed her, standing at the front of the cathedral for all to see, and he had the lowering thought that perhaps the real truth was that he hadn't dared kiss her in private.

Because she was far too potent, and kissing her packed a hard punch.

Gianluca had the most astonishing thought then, and again now. He actually wondered if he'd kept himself from touching her all this time because he knew that once he started, he wouldn't stop.

As if he was a slave to his own desires the way his parents had been.

It was insupportable.

"It's more that my cousin intends to marry for different reasons," Helene was saying, with charming diplomacy. "She has a different take on the enterprise, that's all, and is not certain that she can fully support how we are going about it."

"The history of the world is filled with examples of marriages like ours," he told her, perhaps more repressively that he might have done had he not been questioning himself in real time. "It is not until recently that such arrangements were viewed with suspicion instead of acceptance."

"But were they happy?" Helene smiled when his gaze came to hers, perhaps too sharply. "I am, naturally, transported with nothing short of joy, Your Majesty. Gianluca," she amended as his brows drew together. "It is my cousin who worries that if a couple does not start in a state of tested and true happiness that they can only find themselves miserable."

"Your cousin sounds silly," he replied matter-of-factly. "For even a few moments of research instead of reckless feelings would make it clear to her that when it comes to stability, arranged marriages are more successful. Precisely because the union is not based on such odd notions as happiness or romantic attachment. And our union, Helene, must last. It must stand all tests, of time and trial alike."

He lowered his voice as he said that, lest anyone overhear and imagine there was already trouble, but Helene only nodded.

"I remember what you told me in Provence. No scandals. No separations. One smooth, unified front at all times, forever." She held his gaze as she said that. "I agreed to those terms."

She had. They had been walking in a field

of gold and purple and the sun had seemed to seal the bargain they were making, so solemnly, out where they were nothing but a woman and a man. He could not have said why the way her cousin looked at him got under his skin.

He could not recall ever being quite so prickly before. He could not say he cared for it.

As other couples took to the floor when the music changed, and he was once again called upon to perform for his public, Gianluca found himself questioning that moment over and over.

As if it mattered far more than it should.

And as if he really ought to have been paying closer attention to why it felt that way—

But finally, after an eternity of duty, it was time for him to take hold of his bride and leave the reception behind.

Like everything else about this very public wedding, there were stages to the departure. Everything had to be properly photographed, recorded, and disseminated to the papers, the news shows, and all the rest of the industries that fed like parasites off of his position. A ruler should not be a celebrity, to Gianluca's mind, but that was a battle that had been lost long ago.

But soon enough, the necessary steps had all been taken and he and Helene waved for the last time from the balcony of the palace.

And then, at long last, retreated within.

Though they were not alone.

His usual aides surrounded him as they walked, and he nodded along as they filled him in on things that had happened during this long day of celebration that required his comment or signature or merely his attention. When they arrived at the King and Queen's apartments, half of the entourage peeled away and took Helene with them, so that they might prepare her for the next part of the evening.

As was tradition.

Yet there was something in him that wanted to stop them. That wanted to dismiss all the staff, and carry his own wife into his own bedchamber, then strip her out of that gown of hers with his own hands—

But that was not how things were done. And he was not going to start making up his own rules now. That would spit in the face of all he'd attempted to do since he'd taken the throne and, sooner or later, make him no better than the people he least admired.

So he allowed her to be borne off without him, little as he liked it. Then he tried his best to focus on the things his staff were telling him as he strode into his rooms, casting off his own wedding garments as he went.

But focus did not seem to be available to him. Not today.

And it was a relief to dismiss them soon after, so that he could stand there in nothing but his shirtsleeves and his trousers low on his hips, allowing himself a small bit of liquor that he had decided was permissible long ago.

It was one more thing he would not deviate from now, no matter the provocation.

The Fiammettan Royal Palace was a standing pageant of its own history, much of it starring Gianluca's own family. He had grown up here. He had played in all of these rooms, even when instructed not to, and so he knew exactly which doors separated him and his wife now. He could even guess which rooms her aides were moving her through. Readying the new queen for the King's royal pleasure.

And he was glad, then, that he had taken this moment to himself, because there was a howling thing in him—that brazen hunger—that he was just as happy to keep to himself. So that he might wrestle it under control here, alone, when no one might suspect it lurked within him.

So that he could pretend it did not.

He and Helene had talked about their wedding night, obliquely. He was well aware that in some marriages like theirs, sex was not assumed. That it was something to be worked up to, or perhaps suffered through when necessary.

But he had walked with Helene on a late summer evening out in the garden her mother had planted and had seen the way she'd blushed when she'd nodded and said that all things considered, she was perfectly happy to do things the traditional way.

His mouth went dry even now, remembering it.

Gianluca told himself it was perfectly reasonable to wish to enjoy this particular part of his duty. For he would execute it either way. If he had found himself a woman who flinched at his touch, well, they were both lucky that they lived in a time where intimate touch was not necessary to build the required bloodline a king needed.

But he did not think that was going to be an issue.

When he heard that faint tap at the door at last, and then the sound of it opening, he waited for one beat, then another. He heard her quick, light feet in the hall, yet still he stayed still, his eyes out a window he hadn't looked through once tonight.

Almost as if he was not entirely sure what his response would be.

Or if he could control it, more like—

But then he stopped trying. He turned.

And she stood before him at last.

His wife. His queen.

His Helene.

They'd taken down her hair so that it waved riotously over her shoulders, but still did not conceal the fact that they'd been left bare. That she wore another bit of soft white, but this one cascaded from tiny straps all the way to the floor and was just transparent enough. Just enough, so he saw the hint of the ripe swell of her breasts and got his first taste of the curve of her hips.

One taste was all it took when her eyes were so wide and so gold, and the smile that she aimed at him seemed to resonate deep within him.

He crossed to Helene and finally took his bride into his arms, then fastened his mouth to hers.

This time, there was no one watching them, so Gianluca stopped pretending that he could control any of this.

And so he let himself go.

CHAPTER THREE

THERE WAS NOTHING in the stretch of Helene's life, quietly blooming or not, that could have prepared her for the look on Gianluca's face just then.

Her heart seemed to simply stop, there in her chest, then beat so hard she thought it might knock her flat.

This man who had always seemed so ruthlessly controlled, so stern and so deliberate in all he said and did looked nothing short of... undone.

She barely had time to suck in a small gulp of air before he was there before her and then his hands were on her.

Then his mouth descended to hers.

And then everything caught fire.

And the press of his mouth to hers in the cathedral had shifted things inside her. It had made her wonder ever since if she could handle this, him. It had winnowed all the way through her and then pooled between her legs, so that she'd spent the whole of their reception feeling outside herself, swollen with the need she understood in theory but had never experienced before. Not like this. Not with the memory of those firm lips against hers crowding into her, washing over her, making her question everything.

But now there was no question.

There was only the sleek fire of his mouth on hers and the way he licked his way between her lips, so that one fire became another, the heat building on itself and shaking through her to become another kind of humming all its own.

Louder. Better.

In the Institut, they'd been given all kinds of classes on how best they should treat the loss of their virginities, given that their innocence was likely to be a matter of barter in the marriages girls who grew up there were likely to take part in. They did not shy away from such topics at the school, though, it had to be said, they also did not advertise that particular subject matter much outside the Institut's walls.

Even if you feel overwhelmed, you must lean into it, they'd been advised, in one way or another, by their teachers. *For it is up to you to find your own pleasure, ladies. Whether it is offered to you or not.*

All the girls in Helene's year had been resolute when discussing it amongst themselves. If pleasure was theirs to find, then find it they would. They all read enough. Watched enough. They all knew that what they'd been told was only too true and they would have to assume and then proceed as if it was up to them—

But it had never occurred to Helene that she might find herself in a scenario where locating her own pleasure was not required.

Because *pleasure* was far too tame a word to describe what crested within her, over and over, as Gianluca kissed her. As, again and again, he angled his head to take the kiss deeper.

As if, were it up to him, he might eat her whole.

Everything in her shuddered into the wildest sort of delight at that notion.

Just as quickly, everything seemed to spin around on itself, and it took her a moment to comprehend that he was lifting her from the floor. Something he did so easily and without a pause in the way he was kissing her that it sent another humming thing swirling around inside of her. She leaned into it, still wild over his kisses, and chasing his mouth with her own. Learning with every slide of his tongue, every angle, and even the faint scrape of his teeth.

He set her down on what she assumed was the bed, though she didn't bother to look. All she knew was that he'd set her *apart* from him and, accordingly, she made a soft noise of sorrow.

But it changed into something else halfway through, because she'd never seen him look like this. Gianluca's dark night eyes were a mad heat, and his stern, aristocratic face was changed, somehow. As if he could feel the same wildfire that was eating her alive.

As if it had carved its way into him, too, making him look something like cruel, stark and needy.

Something else she could feel within her, a kind of beckoning.

He moved to stand between her legs, and then reached down, smoothing his heavy palms over her hair, and then, with a look of intense concentration on his face, he set about the task of *learning* her.

Helene could think of nothing else to call it. It was as if he was committing her to memory with his fingers, his hands. And then, as if he wished to make her feel turned inside out, and scalding hot besides, with that mouth of his, too. He started at one temple and eased his way all over her face. Brows, cheekbones. Her nose. Her eyelids.

Then he took his time learning his way along her neck, finding his way to her breasts through the sheer material gown they'd given her to wear. The gown she'd thought made her look silly, a gothic virgin from another age who ought to be chased down a hallway with a candle in her hand—but she had sighed happily when she moved in it, because it was softer than a dream and felt like caresses all over her skin.

Though she understood quickly now that she had no idea what caresses were meant to feel like.

Because Gianluca was a revelation.

He did not make any attempt to lift her gown or find his way beneath it. What he did was urge her back so that she lay against the coverlet, sprawled before him. Her whole body shook with every breath she took, while he took his time.

And lit her up.

Gianluca found her navel, the jut of her hip, and then trailed heat over the top of her most private triangle. He glanced up at her then, only the touch of that vast night, and she braced herself—or she surrendered herself—but he only grazed that wet, hot center between her legs as he worked all the way down to her feet.

Leaving her limp and wild and unable to do anything but *shake*. And then, when he reversed direction and started making his way back up, he pulled the gown along with him.

And Helene lost herself entirely.

She simply…poured herself into him.

Into his mouth, arching her back or thrusting her hips forward, whatever he demanded. Whatever felt good, then better, then better still.

He took his time, moving all the way back up to her face again to kiss her all over again. Until it was almost hard to remember that she was naked and in his arms—

But only *almost*.

Gianluca pulled back and seemed to study her once more, and Helene felt that like a touch all its own. But he did not speak. He looked at her, his face as stark and as wild as she felt, before flipping her over and making his way back down the length of her body once more.

This time, when he made it back up again, Helene was shuddering. Sobbing. Clenching her fingers into the coverlet below her, making fists, writhing—so outside herself she wasn't sure, if asked, she would even know where she was.

Nor did she care as long as this man, her husband, was right here with her, working his rough and tender magic.

He left her for a moment and Helene was so dazed with pleasure and longing that all she could do was lie there, her face pressed against the bed, able to do nothing at all but pant. Her head was spinning. Every nerve ending in her body was *exulting*—

The Gianluca's hands were on her again. And

that was even better, because when he pulled her to him she discovered to her great wonder and delight that he was naked too.

And she wanted nothing more than to celebrate this madness, this astonishing and all-consuming wildfire that felt as good as it burned, so she did her best to mimic what he had done to her.

She tried to follow the bold, breathtakingly masculine lines of his body. She explored the flat planes of his chest. She tested the heavy slabs of muscle along with the deep ridges carved into his abdomen, and she savored every taste of him. Faintly salty, his skin smooth and rough in turn, and these unprecedented acts made a new heat move within her.

And then, when she reached it, the jut of his maleness was huge and hot and it made her feel like whimpering.

With a need she had never felt before.

She reached out, not sure if she wished to wrap her hands around the length of him, or maybe follow a darker, hungrier urge to lean forward and put her mouth on him—

But he didn't let her choose.

Instead, Gianluca tipped her back against the soft bed and crawled his way up the length of her body once more. Until he was beside her, stretched out so that she could see almost all of him at a glance.

And for a moment, she felt almost overwhelmed at the sight of him. Of *all* of him.

Because he was so perfect. And because it all seemed so different from what she'd imagined, but was still perfect. There was no question in her mind about that, either.

Gianluca was long and lean, made of a great many muscles, sleek and heavy. She'd never thought too much about the state of a man's chest, but now she found that his consumed her attention entirely. She was fascinated by the dusting of dark hair there and the way it felt against her body when she rubbed herself against him. The way it made a new and darker flame lick all over her.

As if she'd been made for the sheer physicality of this thing they were doing. As if deep within, all along, there had been this need to wrap her naked body around his—only his— so they could rub together like tinder and see what sparked.

He didn't speak. There was something almost stricken about the way Gianluca looked at her as he reached down between them, found the place where she ached for him the most, and drew his fingers through all that heat.

She felt something break inside her, but broken was better still, and so she shook against him as her thighs clenched of their own accord around his questing hand.

He let out a dark, male sound that Helene had never heard before—and yet knew, somehow, was approval. Then he pressed deeper, as if he knew perfectly well that every time he did, a great wave of sensation washed all over her.

He did this again and again, until she felt something rush at her, hot and dark and *his*, until it burst through her and made her cry out.

Then he was rolling her beneath him, holding her thighs apart with his own hips. His dark gaze was all she could see when she opened her eyes, and she didn't look away as he reached down between their bodies to fit the great blunt head of his manhood against her softest heat.

Helene was a chaotic blaze, too wild to bear. She caught her breath. She found herself dragging her lower lip between her teeth as if that might help her survive this. Gianluca's dark night gaze seemed like it was a part of her, as if it was already deep inside her, as slowly—so very slowly—he began to press himself into her.

"You are too big," she whispered, and there it was again, the flash of that smile of his.

"Have patience, *mia regina*," Gianluca murmured in a low voice, as if his throat was too rough for words.

But he was too big. He really was, and Helene couldn't see how *patience* would help any. There was no way he could fit—

Still he pressed in deep, then deeper still.

She threw back her head and tried to ride it through, the stretching, the pressing. She was so soft and the fire inside her was so bright, and all of these things felt as if they were braided together.

As if it was all meant to be this way, the flames burning hot on one side, and the press of pain on the other, yet somehow working together. So that somehow all of it was wildfire and wonder, and she arched into him, surrendering herself to the grip of it. To the inevitability of the way he slid in, so deep, until she felt him kiss up against the very depths of her.

It was as if everything she was, everything inside her, *rippled*.

And then shattered.

And the shattering was its own kind of dance, its own slick and sweet marvel, a wonder all its own. Too magic and too wild for her to do anything but let it take her.

Over and over.

The way he did as he thrust within her, again and again and again.

So that when she fell back into herself anew,

returned from all the shattering, that was all she knew.

Once. Twice.

Until she broke apart once again, so completely that she was little more than a shooting star off there in the cosmos—

But she heard Gianluca's voice, his wild cry of need and wonder as he came with her, and she thought she could stay like that, scattered out there in the stars, forever.

Particularly if he was with her.

She wasn't sure she would ever come back to her own body again, and when she did it felt wrong. As if she was not meant to be solid like this, separated from him in the indignity of flesh and bone.

Not when they could shine. Not when she knew they could dance like that, out where galaxies collided.

It took her a long while to understand how she was even lying there on her side, curled up next to the blazing hot body of the man she'd married. The man she barely knew.

The man whose addictive taste she had in her mouth, even then.

There were no lights on in this great room of his, but there was a fire dancing in the grate, and she liked the way the firelight moved over his skin and hers. As if it was keeping them connected the way no small part of her felt they were meant to be.

Always.

Just as they had been out there in the stars he sometimes carried in his eyes.

But the longer Helene lay there, the more she found herself going over what they'd just done again and again in her mind, so that her heart began to pound all over again. She had been taught repeatedly that it was always best to allow oneself to be led so that one could more easily adapt to whatever might befall her, but surely that didn't apply to *this*. She was lying there, laid out like the grandest sort of meal, and the man had made her his queen. If rank had its privileges, surely she did not need to deny herself ever again.

So Helene shifted, pushing herself up on her hands so she could look down at the King, her husband, there beside her. He lay there with one arm thrown over his eyes, as if he knew the firelight danced over all the lines of his body and made him into art.

And she had found him gorgeous from the start, there was no denying it. But he seemed something more like *celestial* to her now. She leaned down over him, smiling as her hair found him before she did. She let her soft, dark waves trail across the skin of his chest, as if she was using it like a tool.

Because she was following wherever this mad pleasure led, and more, because he liked it. He began making the most fascinating sound, low in the back of his throat, that made that abundantly plain.

Helene pressed her lips to the pulse she found, beating in time with hers, at the base of his neck. And then she simply gave herself over to that beat. To the longing inside of her.

To the magic of this, and every new marvel she uncovered along the way.

She found the corded tendons in his neck entrancing. She followed them down to his collarbone, lost herself for some while in that shoulder and the underarm he was presenting to her with his arm in that upthrust position. And better yet, his bicep.

After a while, she felt drawn to his chest again, and shivered, because she could remember so clearly how all those hair-roughened muscles had felt against the tips of her breasts. She could feel it again now, as if her body was preparing itself.

But that gave her an idea, so she leaned in and found his nipple, teasing it with her tongue until she heard that growl once more.

And then, more exciting still, she felt the way his big, strong hands clenched deep in her hair.

Helene charted her own course down the length of his torso, eventually realizing that she was following the arrow of dark hair that led to that most mysterious part of him. The lower she went, lavishing attention on ridges and thick muscles alike, the more that part of him stirred.

And by the time she got there, he was hard again. And Helene still couldn't quite believe she'd taken all of that, all of *him*, inside of her.

She wanted that again. But first she wanted to kiss her way around the base of his proud length, taking in all the ways he was so different from her. And then, following that urge she'd had before, and remembering all those books she'd read in secret over the years, she licked her way over the velvety tip of his shaft.

That made him make those sounds again, so she did it again. Then again.

Then she leaned in closer and took him in her mouth as best she could. And this time, when his hands clenched deep into her hair, it very nearly hurt in the most surprisingly thrilling way—

But he wasn't stopping her.

On the contrary, he was keeping her there, right where she most wished to stay.

And as he did, he began to tell her precisely what to do.

His voice was low and certain, a current of

dark, hot glory that wound around her and into her and held her tight as surely as his hands did, still sunk deep into the waves of her hair.

Helene thought she'd never felt more alive than she did now, with his hands on her and that male part of him surging over her tongue as if every single part of her was finally working precisely as it should.

And she had been taught to eat the finest foods. Drink the most exclusive wines. She'd been trained to have an exquisite palate, but none of that tasted like anything to her. There was only the taste of him. The sheer, dizzying, hot and hard *taste*—

Gianluca groaned out his release, then, and flooded her mouth, and that taste took her over— far better and hotter, saltier and more *him* than before.

For a moment, all she could hear was the sawing of his breathing, raw and loud. It took her long moments to recognize that she was trembling everywhere, her heart drumming wild in her chest, and she was once more slick and hot between her legs.

When he moved, she thought he might be about to do something about that. Instead, he rolled from the bed and looked back at her, the firelight making him seem almost soft, almost kind, though he did not taste like either.

He said nothing. He only bent down and swept her up into his arms.

Helene thought then that she would let him carry her anywhere. She trusted him completely. She let her head fall to his shoulder and watched him, not wherever they were going. He was a view that she imagined she would never tire of.

What a sweet magic this was that she would not need to try.

It took her a moment to understand where they were when he set her down on her feet, and she had to bite back a smile, as it seemed so incongruous to her that a mighty king did something as prosaic as reach into the great glass enclosure before them to turn on the water for his own shower.

Like anyone else.

Gianluca pulled her in with him, picked up a whisper-soft cloth, and stood her on one of the benches as he tended to her. He washed every part of her with the same focus and intensity, until the washing itself became a sensual pageant all its own.

Until Helene had her head tipped back, eyes nearly closed, as he began to use his hands instead.

She gasped a bit as he lifted her up. Then more as he pressed her against the side of the great shower enclosure, then hoisted her higher still, until she had no choice but to wrap her thighs around his neck and then reach out to grip the nearest showerhead—because he was gripping her bottom in his hard hands while he used that devastating mouth of his to lick his way deep between her legs.

And for a long while after that, it was all shooting stars and sheer delight.

She came apart again and again, riding his tongue and the sweet torment of his jaw and that *focus*. Then he slid her down the length of his sleek, wet body until he could thrust himself deep within her once again.

Only when they were both limp and hoarse did he slide them both down to sit on the floor of the shower together. The hot water pounded all around them, but the sound of his thundering heart beneath her ear was louder by far. Helene closed her eyes and let her head fall to his shoulder, thinking she might slip off into sleep and stay there for half a lifetime or so.

She still felt that way, sleepy and dreaming, as he toweled her off and carried her back out to the bed. She was barely aware of it when he tucked her in, then sprawled out beside her, but there was a small part of her that resented that her first night with a man was occurring *right then* and she was too spent to truly experience it…

But Helene woke up quickly enough sometime much later when he pulled her on top of him in the dark and taught her new ways to break apart and burn.

When she woke up again, there was light outside the windows and she was alone in the wide bed. She stretched where she lay, feeling new and intriguing twinges in all the different parts of her body. And she was smiling as she sat up, then finally looked around the King's grand bedchamber, which had clearly been decorated to announce precisely who lived here. It was an impressive sweep of art, sculpture, ancient furniture, and the sort of resonant colors that she had learned in school were meant to softly underscore power and might.

It wasn't until she tottered off to the bathroom, blushed at the sight of that shower enclosure, then walked back into the bedroom that she realized the windows were doors that let out onto a balcony. And more, that there was a figure out there in what had to be a rather bitter January cold.

Gianluca.

She pulled one of the quilts that had ended up in a heap on the floor around her like a cape, and pushed her way out through the door. Alpine air bit at her, in a harsh rush, and her breath deserted her. She could see it.

Her husband stood as if he could not feel the cold, but at least he was dressed. He stared out at the view of his kingdom, nestled there before them in the long, narrow valley that was the heart and soul of Fiammetta, and all Helene could think was, *This is the life we get to live*.

She opened her mouth to say it to him, too, but something in his stillness stopped her.

Gianluca did not turn around to greet her. And somehow, she felt that everywhere. Like a bit of foreboding.

Maybe more than a bit.

And when he did turn, it was as cold as the air around them and with far more bite.

Even before he spoke.

"I thought that the rules were clear from the start, Helene," Gianluca said, and his voice made the cold winter morning so high up this mountain feel balmy in comparison. His black eyes seemed fathomless. There was no star in sight. "You were supposed to be a virgin."

CHAPTER FOUR

HELENE WAS EVEN more beautiful with the morning light pouring all over her, making her eyes sparkle and her cheeks get pinker in the mountain air. She looked regal, standing there in nothing but a quilt that looked as if she might be wearing royal robes. She was picture-perfect.

She was beautiful, she was the Queen of Fiammetta, and she was a liar.

How had he missed all the signs? The way her mouth dropped open now, the way his mother's always did when it was convenient. Her eyes going wide, as if she was in shock.

How had he married his mother when he had gone to such great lengths to make that impossible?

Helene opened her mouth, then closed it. Then she tried again. "What?"

Gianluca shook his head. "Is that the best you can come up with? I felt certain you were far more imaginative."

He had woken in something as close to a panic as he had ever felt. He had bolted upright in his bed, rumpled and still warm. And he had stared down at the woman sleeping there beside him, his wife and queen, curled up like the very picture of innocence.

But the entire night that they had spent together suggested otherwise.

Had he dreamed that unpleasant truth? Or was it simply that he woke with that longing for her heavy in him all over again when that was not like him? He had always been as measured in his bed as anywhere else in his life. Not for Gianluca the tyrannies of emotional involvement with anyone, for hadn't he witnessed, personally, where it all led?

He knew that misery all too well.

Images he knew were not nightmares, not quite, rolled through him. His mother claiming her favorite stage, loud sobs and the destruction of hapless objects while his father raged at her, in his insulting, belittling way—

All while Gianluca tried his best to disappear, right where he stood.

He had vowed he would never ransom off his reason to his emotions. He knew too well where it led.

Do yourself a favor, his father had sneered at him once, over a sea of shattered things that

Elettra had hurled at him in one of the private salons. *Find a queen who does not simply aspire to the crown, but knows how to wear it.*

Gianluca thought he'd chosen so astutely. He had not rushed. He had done his research. And still this had happened.

Surely no innocent could have participated the way she had last night. It defied all reason.

When he had first awoken he had tried to find a reason. Any reason at all, but he couldn't convince himself that the woman who had taken him so enthusiastically so many times was not only a technical virgin, but *untouched.*

At first he had felt a deep rage that he could not fully identify. It did not seem clean and righteous like the fury he had always felt toward his parents. It had taken him some time before he'd understood. This was betrayal.

And then the rage made sense, much more sense than that yearning that had sat on him so heavily.

It was, for a few scant moments, even a kind of *relief.*

That was what got him up and out of the bed. He'd paced around the bedchamber as the new day dawned, trying to think his way into a solution for what had happened here. Her betrayal.

He kept repeating that to himself. *Her betrayal.*

But no matter how he tried to think around it, the damage was done. He had married her. He had claimed her as his queen in front of the whole kingdom.

She had not only made him a liar, she had seen to it that he was now participating in an unlawful activity. He, the King. He, Gianluca San Felice, who had long prided himself on his unimpeachable character—the antidote to his parents.

He had to assume that this had been her plan all along. And so, even though it had not been fully dawn, he'd woken up his aide and demanded that her background be investigated. Again. And far more comprehensively.

"As you wish, Your Majesty," his aide had said. "But our initial investigation was remarkably thorough."

"Not thorough enough," Gianluca had retorted.

And then, because he refused to act as if *he* could not control his temper when that had never been an issue for him before now, he'd taken himself out of the bedroom where his beautiful, treacherous wife slept on. He stalked through his apartments until he reached the room set apart for his personal gym. He threw quite a lot of weight around and then he put in a great many miles.

All of that and yet he felt that great betrayal claw at him all over again at the sight of her.

"Step inside," he ordered her, when all she did was gape at him. "Unless it is part of your plan to experience hypothermia when you have only just managed to lie your way into the crown of Fiammetta."

"My plan? Did you say I *lied*?"

She sounded baffled. And he studied her, because she had fooled him. He, who prided himself on his ability to take the measure of any person he encountered at a glance. He, who had always been praised for his cool head and his ability to cut through so much of the pomp and drama that surrounded Fiammettan politics.

Gianluca had come to stand out here in the cold because there was nothing like a high alpine winter to clear the head. And he had decided that the fault must have been in that longing he'd felt for her. She must have known. She must have discovered his trick of taking a first, unobserved look and played on it.

This woman had managed to manipulate him, something he would have sworn—he *had* sworn—could not be done.

Even now he could not believe how credible she seemed. How utterly believable. She walked back inside, then began to shiver as if it was only then, back in the warmth of the bedchamber, that she'd realized how cold she'd really been. It was a fine little detail that he might have thought proved her innocence on any other morning.

But he had been here all of last night. He had been lost in her, completely out of his head with that driving, impossible lust, and she had met him at every kiss, every thrust.

Gianluca knew better, little as he wanted to.

She went and stood near the fire that was not quite banked, keeping her back to it as if she did not dare turn her back to him.

"I don't understand what you're talking about," she said when all he could do was glare at her, trying to see *into* her. Her voice was even. *Careful*.

He had the fleeting notion that she was speaking to him as if she expected him to explode and was attempting to minimize the damage. She was *managing* him. Gianluca would have objected to that, too, but he also could feel that he was the most unsettled he had ever been.

Though he did not *explode* the way both of his parents always had.

He folded his arms over his chest and made certain that his voice was as frigid as the weather outside. "It is an ancient law," he bit out. "Outsiders are forever calling this law archaic, but the truth of the matter is that it brought peace to this kingdom when all the rest of Europe was at war. For many, many centuries. The Kings of Fiammetta learned that marrying virgins was not simply culturally smiled upon, particularly in our less enlightened periods, but kept everything neat and clean, with no need for the sorts of wars that might crop up in other scenarios. Situations in which, for example, enemies or aspirants to the throne might call into question the precision and accuracy of an heir's paternity."

"Thank you."

She didn't sound as if she was offended. Or even particularly upset. She certainly didn't act like she'd been caught out. If anything, she still seemed baffled. He would not like to play poker with her, Gianluca thought bitterly.

Helene continued in that same quiet manner of hers that had lured him in the first place. "I'm actually familiar with the laws of Fiammetta, to some extent. I thought you knew that the palace made certain I was tutored in the intricacies of your country's traditions and a great many of its laws since almost the moment you proposed."

"The virginity of the Fiammettan queen is of paramount importance," he growled at her, sounding nothing at all like his usual composed self, and he blamed her for that, too. "For a great many reasons, not least among them being that the fact you lied means that I have now unwittingly broken the law. You may not care what is right and what is wrong, Helene, but I must assure you that I do. I cannot make the laws if I break them so cavalierly."

She pulled that quilt tighter around her. Her hair was a mess, falling wildly where it would, but it was his mess. He had raked his fingers through her wavy dark hair so many times he could feel the heat of her in the indentations on his palms. He could smell the scent of the shampoo she used. And he hated that despite his fury, he wanted her.

Oh, how he wanted her.

He was hard, achingly so, and having sampled her throughout the night only seemed to make that worse. Because he knew. He wanted to pull her to him. He wanted to throw that quilt to the floor and lay her down on it, then explore her all over again with the daylight washing over her. He wanted to feed her, wash her again, and stay inside her for a week.

For a start.

Gianluca did not understand how a man as civilized as he had always been could turn into such a monster. He had watched his father lose this battle. He had been collateral damage.

He thought, again, of how hard he had worked to disappear—to fade into the walls, the brocaded chairs. How he had done his best to hide in plain sight so that as his parents warred and shouted and threw their missiles at each other, he would not draw fire.

It had not always worked.

And yet here he was.

He supposed he should find a way to be grateful that it was in bringing him to this state that she'd given herself away...but he did not feel anything like *grateful*.

"I don't think I'm following you," Helene said after a moment, and it was some small comfort that her voice was *slightly* less serene. "Is this...? Are you suggesting that I...wasn't a virgin last night?"

The bitter laugh that burst from him then offended him, horrified him, *appalled* him to the core. Because he recognized the sound. Had he not heard his own father make it a thousand times throughout his childhood?

Was this how the war zone began? Was he even now wheeling in the artillery?

His ribs hurt and yet that laugh still hung in the air of the room between them. And he could not seem to keep himself from throwing more words after that sound, as if to make sure he laid down enough cover fire. "Are you suggesting that you were? After that performance? Please spare me the act, Helene. It's too late now."

"Performance?" Her mouth opened, then

closed. "You thought that I…? That it was…a *performance*?"

She seemed to sway slightly on her feet, and though he wanted to reach out to steady her, he could not trust himself to touch her. Not when he knew she was naked, and all he needed to do was unwrap her like the most delectable gift…

Where is your vaunted control now? he demanded of himself, but he had no answer.

"Gianluca." Helene was whispering now. "I can't understand any of this."

"You gave yourself away," he said softly, and even though he knew better, he closed the distance between them.

And he didn't mean to touch her, because surely he should not even *wish* to touch her, but without his meaning to reach out at all his hands were smoothing over her hair.

Almost tenderly.

Though he did not feel anything like tender. "You gave yourself away again and again."

She frowned, and swallowing seemed to take her a moment. "What is it you think I have done?"

He made himself drop his hand, but he could not seem to step back. He, who had long considered his will stronger than iron, *could not* do it. And all she did was gaze back at him as if he was the one hurting *her*. "I will find the truth.

You must know this. I will dig up your lovers, one after the next, if it takes me a lifetime."

"My lovers?" She sounded as if she wanted to laugh, but didn't. Instead she searched his face, her eyes as gold-tipped as he remembered, and how was that fair? Surely he could have imagined at least that. "What lovers do you imagine I have taken? And when would I have enjoyed these trysts? Everyone knows what the Institut is like."

Helene pulled in a breath as if this conversation was upsetting her—but he could not let himself be pulled in by this act of hers. Not again. He could not let her continue to deceive him. He did not yet know what he was going to do about the initial deception that had made him as much of a liar as she was, tainted as he must be by his association with her if anyone were ever to know.

"Maybe you actually don't know what the Institut is like," she corrected herself when he didn't speak. "So I'll tell you. Even if I had wanted a battalion of lovers, there were none to be found. There were guards, but they were never allowed inside the buildings where the students reside. And even if they bypassed the rules, they would regret it, as we are monitored night and day. Your country is not the only place in the world obsessed with something as silly as virginity."

"You think it's silly." Gianluca leaped on her words as if they were evidence. A smoking gun she'd thrown down in the middle of the floor. "Is this why you chose to deceive me? You thought you could trick me and the whole of my country besides because you think our ways are *silly*?"

Helene blew out a breath and closed her eyes for a moment. But only for a moment. Just long enough for Gianluca to start talking himself into reaching out for her once more, as if that might shift the weight of this betrayal inside him. If the great ball of it, dread and shame alike, might ease if she helped him hold it—

But that was a new, terrible madness.

He was very nearly delighted when she opened her eyes again and focused on him, though he found himself less pleased that there was something like the light of battle there. As if she'd found something within her, something resolute.

Not that heavy wedge of concrete she'd left in him.

"I have not deceived you in anything," Helene said, distinctly. But then she wavered, there as he watched, and he couldn't stand that either. That was how his hands ended up on her shoulders. There was an acre of fluffy down stuffing between his palm and her skin. It was the same as not touching her. "But if I had… How was it—exactly—that you decided I was lying to you?"

Gianluca could not let go of her, no matter how many times he ordered himself to do so at once. It infuriated him.

He was Gianluca San Felice. His parents had proven themselves unworthy of the roles they'd held, but he had always been made better. Stronger. He had always had the utmost faith in his righteousness above all things.

And yet this woman seemed to cast some spell upon him that made him question the fundamental truths of who he was. She made him wonder if he even cared about those things when he more than *cared.* He had built back the trust of his people by being, always, nothing short of a paragon.

Not a saint. He would never call himself that, but he did his level best to get as close as a man of flesh and blood could.

He told himself to step back, but he didn't.

Proving once and for all how saintly he was not.

And so, instead, he drew his fingertips down one side of her lying face, still marveling at the silken heat of her soft skin. At that generous mouth of hers that had pleasured him so intently that he was sure he could still feel the scalding hot clasp of sweet seduction on the hardest part of him…

Damn the woman to hell.

"You are meant to be untouched, untried," he gritted out at her. "Instead, last night made it obvious in every possible way that you have been put through your paces in a great many beds before mine."

And then he didn't have to worry about whether or not he could stop touching her, because Helene jerked herself back and out of his grasp. "I beg your pardon. *Put through my paces?* First of all, slut-shaming does not look good on any man, especially not a king. Second, I'm not a horse. What I am and always have been is an avid reader with an excellent imagination. I'm sorry if my enthusiasm offended you. I'm sure that will never be an issue again."

For reasons he couldn't fathom, Gianluca hated the fact that there was distance between them, even though he knew it was better that way. Even though he should have taken a kind of refuge in the fact that she dared speak to him like this, suggesting that *he* was the one at fault.

It was an outrage, and perhaps that was why he moved closer to her, curling one hand to cup the nape of her neck. He pulled her to him once more. "Your enthusiasm was overdone, Helene."

"Or perhaps the great King has never met an

enthusiastic woman before," she shot back with a hint of temper that shocked him, coming from her. "Is that the kind of man you are, Gianluca?"

"Have you no conscience at all?" His voice was low, then. Soft. Deadly. "I took you into that shower expecting that I would have to wash your virgin's blood from your thighs, but there was none. How do you explain this?"

"My deepest apologies," she said, her dark eyes narrowing with another helping of that temper that he would have sworn had been bred out of her long ago. "I didn't realize that the expectation was that we would wave stained bedsheets from the ramparts of the royal palace. I regret to inform you that hymen is not a conscience, despite a great many fevered fantasies, most of them male. And I have ridden far too many horses in my time to expect that there be much to mine, anyway." She leaned in as if about to tell him a secret, but mockingly, and he should have hated this arch version of her. He should have, but he did not. "Fun fact, that doesn't mean I lost my virginity to a horse. Something I would have thought did not need clarification, but then, this has been a deeply surprising morning already."

There was a part of him that wanted to believe her.

Desperately, in fact.

But Gianluca had already seen a game like this unfold. He'd been raised in the middle of it, forever used as a scapegoat, as ammunition, and even, on occasion, as straight cannon fodder.

He took a step back. Then another. "Virgins do not behave as you did."

And he thought that landed on her like a blow, because she jerked, quickly. Then held herself still.

It felt like a blow and he should have gloried in it, but instead it made him feel small. It made that heavy weight in him seem to press down harder.

"And you're the expert on virgins, are you?" Helene's voice was cooler now, more distant. But her eyes flashed even hotter. "Because it seemed pretty clear that you're not one yourself."

"What clued you in? Was it, perhaps, a certain level of enthusiasm that made it clear it was not my first time?"

"This is an unproductive argument." And though Helene's voice was not precisely even, she lifted her chin and stood her ground. Under other circumstances, he might have admired it. "If you require proof, I can't give it to you. It seems silly to me that you have a law on the books but no way to ensure compliance one way or the other. I'm afraid you're simply going to have to believe me."

"What I believe," he said, and then he was moving toward her once more, as if he could not control himself at all. As if he'd lost that ability entirely at some point last night. "What I *know* is that you are a liar. You deceived me, utterly. And I may not know how you did it, but I will find out. It is not only your lovers I will uncover but your objectives. And you can be sure that whatever they might be, you will not achieve them."

He was close enough now to see the way her eyes flashed. And worse still, to smell himself on her skin.

That need, that *hunger*, nearly ate him whole.

"What if you're too late?" she threw back at him, sounding very nearly reckless, another thing he would have said she was incapable of. "What if the whole of my objective was to be your queen. Now what?"

He growled something at her, not certain he even managed to form words. But it didn't matter, because Helene—who he would have said had no temper to speak of—seem consumed with it now. She pushed herself closer to him, gripping that quilt around her like a set of royal robes.

"Will you divorce me, Gianluca? Call for an annulment? What if, even now, your child is within me? Will you be the first divorced, single father king to ever sit on the Fiammet-tan throne? Will your ancestors rise from their graves in protest?"

"Don't tempt me."

"Then why wait?" She turned and made to sweep toward the door. "Let's tell the world right now. Gentle subjects, we consummated the royal marriage, but it was too…*enthusiastic,* so the Queen must clearly be a whore." She threw a scathing sort of look over her shoulder, but it only made her more beautiful. It only made him harder. It only *hurt.* "Would you like to announce it to the populace or shall I?"

And he did not know if she tripped over her own quilt or if he was reaching out for her anyway, but one thing and another, Helene was in his arms.

Where some part of him insisted she belonged. Even now.

And nothing had changed, even though everything had.

She was sleek and glorious, lush and magic.

He could not stop himself. He was not sure he wished to try.

And she looked at him as if she wanted to murder him, but she pressed her mouth to his instead.

As if they had always been at war.

As if they always would be.

As if a war like this was his true birthright.

They came together in a fury, there on the floor of his bedchamber, that quilt and his clothes only pushed aside so he might thrust inside her again and again and again.

But he couldn't tell if she cried out or he did when that wildfire between them burned them whole.

Only that both of them were lost.

CHAPTER FIVE

AT FIRST HELENE thought that it would be all right.

They would have to talk it all through, of course. They would have to unpack whatever it was that had made him hurl accusations at her like that, and it would likely be an unpleasant discussion given how raw he seemed.

But she was, at heart, an optimist.

After all, she'd been raised on a steady diet of fairy tales.

And as they lay there in a pile of his clothes, sprawled out across that quilt, she tried to focus her gaze on the ceiling far above, festooned with near-operatic moldings. She felt she could relate to the feeling of a good aria, as she tried to catch her breath.

She told herself that *surely* it wouldn't feel even better than it had before—and last night had been truly spectacular—if it was all going to go horribly wrong.

But it turned out that she was wrong about that. Because even though she'd managed her father's moods for most of her life, she wasn't prepared for Gianluca.

"Are you ready to—" she began when he stirred beside her, then stuttered over the rest of her sentence when he pinned her with that dark gaze of his. "T-talk now?"

"About what?" he asked, though the question was clearly rhetorical. "What else can be said about this travesty?"

Maybe, she admitted to herself privately, the trouble here was that she wasn't used to feeling quite so vulnerable.

Gianluca stormed away, leaving the *travesty* that was her behind. Naked and reeling and on a quilt on the floor, still trying to find meaning in the moldings. Helene sat up gingerly, not sure that she'd expected something quite so swift and overpowering and brutally, wonderfully sensual.

Then again, she also hadn't expected to be called a liar who had broken Fiammettan law because she had enjoyed her wedding night.

"A subject they really should have covered at the Institut," she said out loud, mostly to see if she could still speak—or if that lump in her throat that she was trying to pretend wasn't growing had taken over entirely.

She climbed up off the floor. Then it took some doing to pull up that quilt after her and wrap it around herself once again. But she could hear her mother's cheerful voice in her head.

"But of course we do the hard things the same way we do the easy, mon chou. *One step at a time, that is all. One little step and then the next."*

Helene thought that it was possible that if she allowed herself to stop going one step at a time, that terrible vulnerability that yawned open inside her might consume her, and she had no idea what might become of her then. Because she had planned for so many different outcomes, but not this one.

She had not expected to like him so much. She had not expected to *want* to throw herself into this marriage the way she had. It had all seemed *charmed,* if she was honest with herself now. As if her mother had been looking after her all this time and had sent her a King Charming to make good on all those happy-ever-after stories she'd told when Helene was little.

Maybe Helene should have remembered that the focus of an Institut graduate was never happiness, but harmony.

They weren't the same thing at all.

That yawning thing inside her seemed to get bigger and heavier, and she really was afraid that if she gave in to it, it would never stop. So she took a moment and tied her hair back from her face, knotting it on the back of her head. She took a few moments to search around for the nightgown she'd worn so briefly last night.

She made herself breathe. In. Out. Again.

And she had only just settled herself in one of the chairs by the fire, no longer naked and marginally calmer, when the doors were flung open and a set of palace aides streamed in.

Her aides, Helene realized belatedly. The same group of women who had dressed her last night, though that felt like a lifetime ago now. They came in and swept her out of the King's bedchamber, chattering happily.

"The day is fine and bright, if cold," one said in French. "Surely this must be in celebration of our new Queen!"

"What a romantic wedding!" cried another in Italian. "The King and the Queen were all that is elegant and beautiful—all the papers are swooning!"

"It has even been picked up all the way in America," said another in German. "They had to show the location of Fiammetta on a map, naturally, but this does not take away from the fact your special day received international notice, Your Majesty."

Helene was surprised to find this all a comfort, as she was not called upon to respond in any way. They marched her off the way she'd come, down that long hall that snaked along an interior wall of this part of the palace for the sole purpose of letting the King and Queen come and go from each other's apartments as they chose. Or did not choose.

It was possible, Helene thought, that she might stick a chair in front of her side of the door forevermore.

Though no matter how entertaining it was to think such a thing, she knew she wouldn't.

"There's a bath drawn and waiting, Your Majesty," one of the women said. "We've taken the liberty of sprinkling in some soothing herbs. A lovely soak might be just the thing."

"That sounds perfect," Helene murmured.

And it was indeed a lovely soak in an epic sort of tub could have held a family or two, placed advantageously in a set of windows that looked out across the whole of the Fiammettan mountain valley. A place she'd expected to call home. And now...

Somehow, *home* wasn't the word that came to mind.

When she was pickled straight through she got out of the bath, expecting the staff to descend upon her once more. She imagined all kinds of things they could do now. Perhaps march her off somewhere, having packed up all her things, so she could be divorced? Or arrested? Or whatever it was Gianluca thought was going to happen now that he'd decided she was a liar and a travesty.

But instead they led her into one of the smaller rooms, bright with the winter sun, where she ate a solitary breakfast. And rather hated herself for it, all things considered. Because surely, after what happened between her and Gianluca, she should have had no appetite whatsoever. She should have been wan and pale, better suited to a fainting couch than the hearty meal—*"A great favorite of the field hands, Your Majesty,"* one of the aides told her when she asked for more coffee and a second helping of sausages—that she tucked into as if she hadn't eaten in weeks.

Though she hadn't, really. There had been too many dress fittings and too much nervous fussing on the part of her father and too many dire warnings about appearing in photos and appearing on television and how Helene was going to have to get used to thinking about the end result on film, not what she might see in a mirror. That had rather dulled her appetite.

Then, of course, there'd been a great deal of physical activity last night, and none of it—despite what Gianluca seemed to think—anything she was used to at all. That would make anyone hungry, she thought.

"And if I'm soon to be kicked out of the Kingdom, I might as well build up my strength," she told herself. Particularly if it involved going over those towering mountains into Italy.

But she couldn't eat forever. And by the time the afternoon rolled around, she had napped and showered again and had a huge lunch, and found herself…bored silly.

Something that had never occurred to her before, in all her life, because there had always been an inescapable *thing* bearing down on her. Her mother's sickness and death. Her father's ambitions. Her inevitable graduation from school that would mean it was time for her to actually do the things Herbert had talked about all her life.

But now she'd done all those things. She'd actually thought yesterday that she'd won some kind of lottery. She'd been so *proud* that she'd managed to make all the things she'd dreaded, but had been resolved to do anyway, work for her.

"You know what pride goes before," she muttered to herself after her sixteenth turn through the Queen's apartments.

They were expansive and luxurious. She had rooms for everything and anything. Her own gym, her own media room, a selection of salons and lounges, studies, an office, a small kitchen should she wish to have things on hand rather than having to ring down to the palace kitchens, her own library, two separate art galleries, a balcony that it was too cold to investigate fully. It was far nicer than any other place she'd ever stayed.

But she was antsy and filled with dread, which meant she couldn't concentrate on anything. And she didn't want to sit still—that way could only lead her to that pit of vulnerability and something too much like despair deep within.

Better to call it *boredom* and *do something* about it.

Happily, Helene knew a thing or two about the Fiammettan palace that was now her new home, because she'd been taken on a great many official tours of the place. First when she'd visited here after she and Gianluca were engaged, and then, as the wedding drew closer, when she'd lived in one of the royal residences on the palace grounds and her tutors had used the palace's many riches as a part of their lessons.

That meant that she knew that in addition to the grand library that was sometimes open to the public and better resembled a ballroom than a place of quiet study, there were any number of smaller libraries placed here and there in the palace's many wings. As if various royals in the past had felt it was beneath them to walk to the larger, more centralized library and so had created their own.

Fiammettans, Helene had discovered, liked to have more than one of everything. More than one official language. More than one city that called itself the capital of the Kingdom, depending on the season. Just like there was more than one door that led out of every room in every official building in the Kingdom.

Including, she discovered, the Queen's rooms.

It really did pay to nose about, trying every door. Including the one that she knew led into that shared hallway between her rooms and Gianluca's rooms, which she was somehow unsurprised to find locked.

Against her.

For a moment she stood there, staring at the door handle, while that yawning thing inside her seemed to swallow her whole—but no.

It wasn't going to be a locked door that was the end of her. She refused.

At first Helene thought that perhaps this meant he'd locked her in, effectively putting her under palace arrest, but soon after she found the door that opened up into the hallway from the Queen's little kitchen and it opened easily enough.

By this point, happily, she was no longer dressed in a quilt pulled from a bed or a night-gown that she never wanted to lay eyes on again. One of the things her aides had showed her in her daze this morning was her own vast ward-robe. Room after room of it. All of her own clothes, imported from her father's house, and then entire sets of pieces she'd never seen before.

Gifts for you, Your Majesty, her aide had said with shining eyes.

From the King, who loves me so much? Helene had asked.

And had only smiled serenely when the woman looked at her curiously, suggesting that Helene's tone had been a touch too sharp.

In any case, she been able to ignore any *gifts* and dress herself instead in her favorite pair of jeans, the ballet flats that never failed to make her feel both comfortable and elegant at once, and an extremely cozy sweater that held her like the hug she desperately needed.

If there was a dress code for royal travesties, someone was going to have to tell her so.

Helene was out the door and out wandering the halls of the greater palace complex before she realized how strange it felt to be walk-ing around this place dressed the way she had dressed any number of days at the Institut, or in her father's house, back when she had felt that achieving a feeling of not actively hating her life was the best Herbert Archibald's daughter ever *could* feel.

Then she had met Gianluca.

She had imagined a whole other universe of potential feelings all summer long.

And she had married a king, become a queen, and been accused of being a deceitful whore all in the course of the last twenty-four hours.

Yet here she was. Hair twisted back out of her way, her favorite clothes on, and all on her own, again.

Helene told herself, repeatedly, that this should feel like a comfort.

All the comforts of home, in fact.

The other good news about having married the King was that she been given access to her mobile phone again. She suspected it was monitored, but that was what was so funny about all of this. In the sense of not being funny at all. She didn't really care if Gianluca read every text she'd ever sent anyone. What was he going to find?

She really was exactly as innocent she claimed to be.

And she really did watch that many videos of cats doing cattish things.

Helene texted Faith as she walked, taking a picture of herself in front of an instantly recognizable painting as punctuation.

Her cousin's reply was immediate.

I beg your pardon, Your Majesty. Dutch Masters and kings? The world really is your oyster.

And for the first time in her life, Helene did not text Faith a full recounting of the night before. She did not tell her cousin what she was actually thinking or feeling. In fact, as she stood there staring down at the screen of her mobile, she felt the strangest feeling creep over her, twining with that knot of vulnerability that seemed to pulse deep within.

It was the headmistress in her head once again. *Remember, ladies,* she had said in that crisp manner of hers. *The ideal wife does not share her marital troubles with all and sundry. She is never a source for unscrupulous journalists and she does not take even her closest friends into her confidence on matters pertaining to the private things that go on between men and women, no matter her station. Why?*

Because she has already been bought and sold once already? one of Helene's more bitter classmates, who was not expecting happy ever anything, had replied.

Madame had only smiled in that flinty manner she did so well. *Perhaps, Georgianna. But also because part of her power lies in how she protects her marriage. Men, you see, are so good at making declarations about what it is they want, what it is they demand. They bluster, they bloviate, and in many ways, we must accommodate them. But it is the woman who is the bellwether, like it or not. How she behaves sets the stage for how the world will treat not only her, but the marriage that entirely too many will believe is within her purview to change as she wishes.*

Everyone in Helene's year had dissected that particular nugget and called it utter crap.

But now Helene stood there in the Royal Palace of Fiammetta, her mobile in her hand and her cousin right there on the other end of the text. She could say anything she liked. Faith would believe her no matter what she said, even if it wasn't true. Faith would immediately come in, guns blazing—whether only via text or actually at the palace gates depended on what Helene told her.

Helene knew this without having to type a word.

Or…she could protect her fragile, likely fractured relationship with Gianluca instead.

She sent her cousin a string of emojis that said

nothing at all, then slipped her mobile into her back pocket before she could ask herself why.

It wasn't until she'd located what likely qualified as one of the so-called "pocket libraries"—though it was large and featured a great many window seats that let in the snow as it began to fall—that she understood that it wasn't the headmistress's discussion of various kinds of subservience that made her want to protect this.

Whatever *this* was.

It was her mother.

Her lovely Mama, who had maintained until the end that she was happy. She had insisted on it. And she had never, to Helene's knowledge, *ever* told another soul about the things Herbert did that an objective observer might find unkind.

She had even defended him to Helene herself.

Why didn't you marry a Prince Charming? Helene had asked, artlessly enough, when she was too young to know better.

Her mother had held her there, snug in her lap, and so it was only now in retrospect that Helene thought that the smile she'd given then was sad.

But I did, mon chou, she had said. *That is the thing about Prince Charmings, you see. Sometimes it is only their chosen princess who can see them for who they truly are. Don't you worry. You'll know.*

Looking back, Helene did not think her mother truly believed that Herbert was any kind of Prince Charming. But she had protected him anyway.

He had kept her, clothed her, allowed her as much time with her child as she wished, and then he had cared for her when she fell ill. He had protected her, too, in his way.

And Helene did not have it in her to do otherwise.

Or perhaps, she thought later, when she'd found her way back to her rooms with an armful of books so the staff could dress her for a dinner she had assumed she'd be taking on her own, that wasn't the truth. Perhaps the truth was that she was a coward. That she had not wished to face her cousin's reaction if she told Faith what had really happened.

Perhaps she was afraid that a marriage—or her marriage, at any rate—was a fragile thing. And that that telling others the truth of what happened inside it could tear it asunder.

But then she was marched through that previously locked door and down the hall into the King's rooms to find herself in Gianluca's private dining chamber. And she rather thought that if there was going to be any sundering, he would do it himself.

He greeted her with sharp, frigid courtesy, dismissed his staff, and then gazed at her as if she was a specimen beneath the microscope that had gone unexpectedly viral.

"I've spent the day considering my options," he told her.

"That bodes well," she replied, which was not the way she had been taught to handle such situations, but there was only so much she could be expected to do. She laced her fingers together in front of her, wishing she had pushed back a bit more when the women had selected the dress she was wearing. It was far too voluminous. It felt like another wedding gown all over again and even though it was certainly not a virginal white, it made her feel…

Well. Too many things and none she liked.

Gianluca stood there by the great windows that let the mountains in, staring at her, and she had the faint notion that if she took her seat he would take his as well, but she didn't. She stared back at him, wondering where that man she thought she was getting to know had gone.

Or how he could read her so wrongly.

She supposed the silver lining in this was, the knot in the deepest part of her aside, that she couldn't feel the sort of shame and horror she supposed she ought to, because it was *that* ridiculous. No man had ever touched her but him. Yet he believed she was as dissipated as the nefarious, likely made-up women the headmistress had always thundered at them to heed as terrible warnings.

Helene almost wished she really had been out there, sewing wild oats with abandon, if she was going to be punished for it either way.

"You have put me in a terrible position and I will never forgive you for it," Gianluca said in that low, cold voice of his. And that might have been a body blow. If she was guilty. "If I divorce or annul you there is not only the fact that I would be forced to share the fact that you inadvertently made me break the law, I would break even more traditions by ruling while divorced. I would appear weak and easily fooled. None of these are options. We will concentrate on the things we can control. We will get you with child."

Helene might actually have flinched. "Excuse me?"

Gianluca did not appear to notice her reaction. "This is what you promised me, Helene. Is it not bad enough that you lied about the part that is actually required by ancient law? Will you now cast aside every other vow you took as well? Will you attempt to undercut my reign with the scandals and tantrums that have sunk many other monarchies in these modern times?"

She could hardly breathe. "And if I do?"

"You will not have that opportunity." He looked grim. But also something like…pleased, she thought. As if he wanted the chance to issue these threats. As if that allowed him the control he clearly wanted so badly. "My grandmother cherished her isolation, and thus built herself a small castle halfway to the Italian border, accessible only by helicopter or a very sturdy mule. It has no contact with the outside world. Know, with every part of you that imagined it was wise to lie to me, that I will think nothing of stashing you there if I must. That I will always do whatever I must to protect this kingdom."

Helene made herself sigh a bit, as if none of this was really affecting her, when that wasn't at all true. But she suddenly thought that she would rather die than let him *see* her. "That sounds a lot like a high school reunion, if I'm honest."

He stared at her for a small eternity. Maybe two. "Do you think this is a joke, Helene? Because let me assure you in the strongest possible terms that it is not."

"I can see that."

And then it took her a moment to realize that the reason her throat felt so strange was because there was a lump in it again, larger than before. And her eyes felt scratchy, as if she'd been hollowed out. Worst of all, that knot in her took up its own sort of humming, and it made her want to do something completely out of character.

Like fall to the floor and sob.

We do the hard things the same way we do the easy, she thought.

And then Helene swept forward in her absurdly oversize gown and seated herself at the place set for her at the table—on a diagonal from the table's head, which it did not take a great chess master to realize was set for the King—and settled herself into place with what she hoped was every appearance of total serenity.

She'd learned that from her mother, too. That when in doubt, simple rituals could carry an awkward moment and were often far more effective than engaging in a scene.

Though as she sat there, her hands folded in her lap, pretending not to sneak glances at him from beneath her demurely lowered eyelids, she had the distinct impression that he might have preferred a scene, after all.

That this was him, throwing one.

There was something in her that wanted to rise to meet it, the way she'd met every touch, every caress, every moan last night.

But everything in her balked at that.

And this wasn't anything she'd been taught. It was something deeper. Some feminine intuition that was all hers, whispering that if she behaved the wanton in this, too, it would prove his point to him.

More, that Gianluca wanted her to do exactly that.

Helene had no intention whatsoever of doing that work on his behalf.

She was aware of him—too aware of him— but still she sat, engaged in what had been known in the Institut as quiet domestic warfare. The province, according to their teachers, of every powerful woman who could not claim the spotlight herself.

If one must be the power behind the throne, Madame liked to say, *it behooves one to know how to wield it to its best effect.*

And that almost made Helene smile. For there had been no point in any of her schooling in how to be *the most aristocratic of all* that it had ever occurred to her that she would end up anywhere near a *real* throne. Just as she hadn't anticipated getting on the wrong side of her new husband so quickly. Surely she had to have set some kind of record.

She thought that his glare intensified when he finally took his seat, likely because she had permitted her lips to curve in wry amusement.

She thought he might lay into her then, but he didn't. Their meal was served with the exquisite perfection that she had come to understand he required in all things. It was not until all the staff withdrew, leaving them to enjoy their food, that he spoke again.

"Just so we're clear," he said forbiddingly, and when he looked at her it *hurt*, "I remain as allergic to even the hint of scandal as ever. There can be no whispers. No rumors. I will know precisely where to look if any appear."

"Happily," she said, attacking her first course with gusto as if she was too hungry to pay any attention to him, "I haven't the slightest idea how to set about starting a rumor. I was taught many things in the course of my schooling, but never that."

He picked up his fork too, but only fiddled with it, that brooding glare hard on hers. The more he glared, the less it hurt. Or so she told herself. Bracingly.

"You've picked up many things indeed," he said, his insinuation unpleasant. Deliberately, she knew. "And I cannot pretend that I have reached any place of equanimity about the deception you have committed against crown and kingdom."

"My sins are vast indeed."

That black gaze of his darkened further, without the faintest hint of starshine. "All I can tell you in the meantime is what we will do to mitigate this crisis."

She did not ask what that was. Instead she allowed the sound of their cutlery against their plates to make a bit of music.

"If we are to sit in such baleful silence at each meal," she said after this went on some while, "and assuming that we will be taking our meals together, which I realize isn't at all certain given your opinion on my character as that would put anyone off their food—"

"This will obviously be viewed as something of a honeymoon phase," he said darkly, as if Helene was personally responsible for such wedding traditions. To add to her list of sins. "Even though we will not take any sort of holiday, we must behave like newlyweds." When she only slid a look his way, he set his fork down and leaned back in his chair. "In other words, yes. We will be taking our meals together. We will have a heavy slate of engagements to introduce ourselves as a working couple to the whole of the Kingdom, and assuming you manage to not embarrass yourself or the crown, you may even have your own. But I suggest you remember that it is nothing but a pantomime. You are on borrowed time."

Helene waved a hand. "Yes, yes. You will have your revenge." It made her feel strong, she could admit, to come so close to laughing when nothing was funny. She thought she had never understood her mother more, for what could be more infuriating to a man who *wanted* to cause upset than…not to seem the least upset? She smiled at Gianluca. "In the meantime, however, it would be so much more pleasant to have a bit of music while we eat, don't you think? To cover up the echoing silence and seething recrimination between us."

"I imagine we will have something," he told her in that same dark way that made her wish, despite herself, that all of this was the way she'd imagined it might be last night. "You can be certain of that."

"Marvelous," she said brightly, tucking into her second course. "In the meantime, I believe you mentioned crisis management. Which involves me playing the role of broodmare, does it not?"

When he laughed, then, it was a dark, grim sort of sound that nevertheless set off explosions and wildfires all over her body. As if, no matter what, they were connected now. They were connected intimately, so that even a laugh like that winnowed all the way down her spine.

Then settled there, spreading until it hummed deep between her legs.

And the only shame Helene felt was that it didn't matter that he thought her a liar. It didn't matter to her body at all. She felt swollen with need, aching with it. Even if, at the same time, she had the distinct urge to take one of the forks lined up so prettily beside her plate and stab him with it.

She didn't know how she could feel so many things at one time for the same person. She didn't even *like* the man very much right now and yet she knew that if he reached over and put his hands on her again, she would melt into his arms. At once.

"You act as if providing heirs to the throne was not your primary purpose all along." Gianluca lifted a brow. "Or were you somehow under the impression that the King of Fiammetta went about looking for a bride with certain requirements for sport?"

Once again, something inside Helene shifted. She couldn't tell what she felt, then. She only knew that it was dangerous. That it seemed entirely too likely to tear her apart.

Steps, she reminded herself. And the only step available to her was to breathe.

And to stay very still, so none of the things inside her *erupted*.

"This is not a love match, Helene," the man who had been inside her in too many ways to count growled at her. "For which I can only count myself endlessly grateful. The good news is that there is no longer any reason whatever to pretend otherwise."

He pushed back from the table then, standing up so swiftly that she was caught first by the grace in the way he moved. And she knew him on a far more intimate level now. But there was also that lurching sort of hope that bloomed in her immediately, because some part of her clearly wished that he would reach for her after all—

But instead, he stalked from the room, as if he could not bear another moment in her presence.

Leaving behind the sort of bone-deep silence that she doubted very much any music could cover at all.

So there was nothing to do but sit there, staring down at her plate, whispering words that seemed to rebound back at her.

"I wasn't pretending," she said, because something in her felt as if it might break into pieces if she didn't say it.

She said it again, then again, to the plate before her and the mountains that pressed in from the night outside.

But it didn't make her feel any better when she did.

CHAPTER SIX

HELENE DIDN'T KNOW a whole lot about typical honeymoons, that having been considered low on the priority list of marital concerns across the board, but she did feel fairly certain that most people did not spend it in as much of a deep freeze as she and Gianluca did.

A deep freeze that had nothing to do with the typically blizzard-like conditions outside, that was.

While the snow fell—and fell and fell—the palace was toasty and warm. Fiammettans were well used to their excessively cold winters and Helene's astonishment at the snow that built up on her balcony rail each morning only made her aides laugh.

This was how she knew that what she viewed as entirely too much winter weather was perfectly normal to them.

She tried to tell herself that the same was true of her marriage. It wasn't as if she had a host of friends who were also queens who she could ask, so for all she knew, this was bog-standard behavior for kings of all kinds.

Helene assured herself it was.

That, too, was comforting. In its way. Since for all his talk of *broodmares*, Gianluca did not touch her that way again. She tried to tell herself it was a *welcome reprieve*, but she knew that was exactly the kind of lie he had already accused her of telling him.

Because every night, her usual staff would walk her back to her bedroom from the King's private dining room and then assist her in undressing herself, as if walking and undressing were activities that suddenly required a team effort now that she had married a king. She supposed it was to remind her that everything she did could be scrutinized, and thus she had better act the part.

As if she had ever *not* acted appropriately in the whole of her life—but then, that was his contention, wasn't it?

What it meant was that it was only when Helene crawled into the Queen's stout and imposing four-poster bed and lay there, staring at the elegantly embellished paneled ceiling, that she could really replay their wedding night.

Over and over and over again.

And admit to herself that it did not feel much

like a reprieve at all that he had taken that away from her. That wonder and heat. That soaring, life-altering delight.

It felt like cruelty.

But that was the nighttime. The first few *days* of their so-called honeymoon, ever cognizant of the fact they were under scrutiny from the palace staff and the typical tabloid spies within, Gianluca insisted—coldly—that they do the kinds of things they had done while courting.

Quote marks implied.

They took walks in the palace gardens, every day the weather was clear enough. When it was not, they toured the palace galleries. They made polite conversation, as if they were very distant strangers. Breathless accounts of these moments made their way into the papers and if they ventured outside, usually with a picture to match.

"I thought you wanted there to be no discussion of anything we do in the papers," Helene said on one of these promenades across the snow-cleared pathways under which, she knew from photographs, glorious flowerbeds waited for spring.

Gianluca shot her a glimmering sort of look as he kept pace with her, in a manner she knew too well the public interpreted as him *hanging on her every word*. "That is not realistic. And that being so, I prefer to offer them the content

I wish to see rather than having them dig up things on their own."

Though he made that sound as if there was a great wealth of digging to be done, and all of it to expose her.

She endeavored to ignore that. "There have been a great many pieces about the Royal Family since our wedding. Takes on history from various viewpoints. I'm enjoying them all, though I keep reading references to your father's *moods* that seem to be nearly in code—"

"Helene." And he was still *glimmering* at her, so she was the only one who could see that he was not hanging on her words. He wanted them to stop. Now. "Unless you see that an article came directly from the palace, you can assume that it is fiction."

Helene only smiled noncommittally, gazed at the snowbanks, and kept her questions to herself for the rest of their walk.

At least these forced interactions were mercifully brief. Perhaps an hour each day of pantomime, and otherwise, Helene was given the run of the palace libraries to do as she would. And it wasn't that spending her days eating marvelous food, reading books, and going on walks—with or without the company of a brooding, furious male—was torture in any real sense. She knew that. In many ways, it was the life she'd always dreamed she might have, having digested every possible version of *Beauty and the Beast* ever made.

It was only that everything felt so *fraught*. And she couldn't help but think this was all a lot of tiptoeing around land mines while hoping for the best.

Instead of worrying about the inevitable explosion, she dedicated herself to the task of answering her own questions. There were very few papers or magazines allowed in the palace, so she scoured the libraries for primary sources when it came to the Royal Family in general and former King Alvize in particular.

Because she couldn't help but think that the key to Gianluca, and his wild reaction to their wedding night, was caught up somehow in those *moods* everyone seemed to know about but no one dared mention directly.

She didn't find much, but what she discovered was that if the staff saw her curled up in armchairs with stacks of old books, no one questioned what she was reading online.

After a week or so had passed, her aides woke her up one morning to announce that it was time she took on her expected royal duties. This meant they shuffled her between tutors again, so that she might learn everything there was to learn about the Kingdom. And more, the historic role of the Queen.

Or rather, the spouse of the monarch, for Fiammetta had enjoyed three queens in its time. One had maintained what was considered a perfect marriage to a man who was perfectly happy to loom about in the background, assisting the throne, which her tutors told her was the sort of marriage Helene should view as her guide. The second queen had ruled only a few short years and had been married to the Prince of a neighboring land, but had died without issue. Throwing the Kingdom into chaos, according to her tutor, who had waxed on about the war that had raged for many years after that short-lived queen's death, as various would-be heirs vied to take their place on the throne.

"This is the one who interests me," Helene said, smiling winningly at her tutor while tapping her finger on the picture of the third queen, who had married as she had been ordered to do. And then, when her prince turned out to have his own aspirations for the throne—and wasn't above a plot or two to get his way—had first had him imprisoned, then assassinated. "It's a bit of a lovely bedtime story to tell the children, isn't it?"

"Your Majesty is very droll," her tutor replied.

Quelling.

But she was curious, not droll. Because all these lessons about historical queens made her think more about the only other queen she knew—from a distance. That being the Dowager Queen Elettra, about whom Gianluca had nothing at all to say. He refused to discuss her.

That left Helene no recourse but a forensic examination of the tabloids. She enlisted Faith's help, claiming she wished only to get to know the way her new family was portrayed over time in the popular imagination.

Faith was only too happy to dedicate herself to the task of tracking down chatrooms and message boards and vitriolic social media threads, but it all painted the same picture. Yes, King Alvize had been a touch moody—if the "palace insider" reports were true, and always in private—but everyone agreed that Queen Elettra's whorish ways *drove him to it*.

It was that word *whorish* that Helene couldn't seem to let go of. It was the universality of the response to Elettra, which she knew by now had to be a specific and deliberate campaign. And not one that benefited the woman in question.

After all, Helene knew a thing or two about being called a whore.

One night, as they departed the palace in the royal motorcade with flags flying, she opted to regale Gianluca with the entire bloody story of his ancestress, the assassin, whom history unfairly called *the Killer Queen*. "She had good reason to do what she did, if you think about it."

"He was the King and she plotted against him, Helene. I think you'll find that's more commonly known as treason."

"He was plotting against her first," she argued. Then smiled when Gianluca raised that brow of his at her. "And you know what they say."

"Be careful who you marry?"

She smiled wider. "Play stupid games, win stupid prizes."

He did not speak to her directly again that night unless it was necessary.

Oh, he put on an act. It was humbling, really, to see how good he was at acting. It made her question every single moment she'd spent in his presence. Had it *all* been an act? Helene had been so certain that despite their circumstances, and despite the arrangements that had to be made for a man in his position—not to mention, the arrangements her father had always intended to make for her no matter if a king turned up or not—there had still been something between them.

The way he had smiled at her, surely, had been real.

If rare.

She was still holding on to that.

"You did well enough," he pronounced on the way home from the gala, the two of them tucked away again in the dark backseat of the limousine. "It is heartening to see that I can depend on you to play the appropriate role. If nothing else."

"I'm very well trained," Helene agreed. Mildly enough. "You should direct any and all compliments to the Institut, however, as this is their entire purpose for existing."

"If I were you," he said, in that dark-night-of-the-soul sort of voice of his that she wished did not make her ache, "I would not be so flippant. I have no reason to think that any of the things I was led to believe about you are true, do I?"

She turned to him as the motorcade sped through the narrow streets of the old city, all cleared in advance to make way for the King and Queen. "I don't think you're in a position to speak on such matters when it turns out that you, apparently, could be an award-winning actor. If I didn't know any better, I would have thought that you were desperately in love with me tonight."

Helene shouldn't have said it like that. That was clear the moment the words cleared her lips, because the look on his face changed. It became darker, deadlier. Or perhaps it was simply that she felt it as it thudded through her, then seemed to squat there inside, a thorny, pulsing thing she really didn't want to look at too closely.

Because she also didn't want to think about the way it had *felt*, circling around a glittering gala on this man's arm, too aware of the way he looked at her. As if he was the besotted yet capable king she'd imagined he would be.

It had been too easy to believe, for a few hours, that they hadn't taken this bizarre turn.

"What you must understand, Helene, is that I will always give my people what they want," he told her. And every word felt like a knife. Like a blade he was specifically aiming directly at her, each syllable precisely uttered to pierce her poor heart.

She made herself smile anyway. "And you think that's what they want? An act?"

"I know what they don't want. My parents' endless operatics, each and every salacious headline making a mockery of the duty they were called upon to perform for this kingdom. My people want a love story, and they will receive one." His gaze made her heart feel even more perforated. "No matter what I have to do."

"It will be a tender love story indeed," she replied, and did not shrink from that gaze, no matter how she might wish to, "and will seem especially so when I am carted off to a mountaintop prison, without my children, to live out my days in isolation."

But Gianluca smiled, and not in the way that made everything around her feel like an endless summer. This was a cruel crook of his lips, nothing more. "You must have more faith in the palace's ability to spin a story, Helene. When they are finished, the Kingdom will rejoice. They will tell the story as if it is our very own Fiammettan fairy tale. Watch and see."

"I believe the palace can spin anything," she replied quietly, and had to take what satisfaction she could from the way his lips pressed together.

That night, she lay in her bed while her body still ached in all these new ways that he had taught her, then taken away from her. He was pretending to love her in public. She was pretending she didn't care that he despised her in private.

And none of that helped with this ache at all.

It was possible that nothing ever would.

Once the tears started, they didn't stop.

Helene sobbed. She sobbed until her head hurt almost as much as her heart. And when she staggered into her bathroom suite, all the mirrors and marble reflected back her own red eyes and swollen face, and she thought, *At least I finally look the way I feel.*

But that was so tragic it made her laugh at herself, and she ran cold water over her wrists for a while until she calmed. Then wet a cloth so she could press it to her eyes.

And when she'd gotten the swelling down a bit, she went back out into the bedroom and wrapped herself in her favorite cloud-like throw that was always folded so neatly over the chair near the fire. She wrapped herself in it, sighing at the touch of warm cashmere against her skin, and then moved over to the windows she could curl up in the window seat and press her face to the cold glass.

It was still January. It was breathtakingly cold. Earlier tonight, as she'd stood outside so briefly to go in and out of the palace and the gala wrapped in warm things, she'd felt the sharp alpine air cut all the way through her. She'd taken a deep, shuddery breath each time, as if she was afraid it would be too cold for her lungs to work.

That was what she felt like now, gazing out at the bright lights of the long, narrow valley that made up the bulk of this kingdom. This kingdom that was now hers, whether the King liked her or not.

And Helene had always considered herself something of an indomitable spirit, but tonight, the self-pity took hold. Hard. Because she had only been said indomitable spirit because she'd always hoped, deep down, that things would end well.

She'd trusted that they would, no matter how they appeared.

But now…was this really what her life was going to be like? This…fakeness in public followed by so much darkness in private? Part of her wanted to get up immediately, snatch up her mobile, and beg Faith to come break her out of here after all.

She considered it logically, and for a long time. It would never work, for a number of reasons. First of all, her cousin was loyal and true, but she was no match for the royal guard. And even if she somehow managed to get into the palace, there was no way she was going to abscond with the Queen. Besides, even if Helene attempted to trick her way out of this, she doubted Gianluca was going to let her traipse off on some kind of holiday anytime soon.

Did queens even take holidays?

And in any case, it wouldn't solve anything. Even if she did run away. Helene and Faith could ski on their bottoms all the way into Italy and set themselves up in a lovely *pensione*, and it wouldn't make her any less the new Queen of Fiammetta. It wouldn't solve her marriage. It wouldn't do anything but give Gianluca more proof, somehow, that she was this person he thought she was. A liar who would also run away from him, thereby causing an even bigger scandal.

Still, she stayed where she was for a long while, her forehead against the glass and her breath a little more ragged that she wanted to admit even to herself. And slowly, that great tide of tears and despair seemed to ebb away.

Helene wrapped herself tighter in her cozy throw and angled herself away from the window, so that the winter cold was no longer pressing into her skin. She pressed her fingers to her eyes, blew out a breath, and then straightened her shoulders.

The truth was, she had spent the entirety of her life learning how to manage a man who never acted as if he cared for her at all. Herbert had been a marvelous training ground in that regard. She had watched her mother do it, then she had done it. And while she couldn't claim that she had actually pleased the man, because he couldn't be pleased at all and certainly not by her, the situation she found herself in here in Fiammetta was nothing new.

The specifics might be different, and more personal, but it was the same old game.

If she looked at it that way, the only problem she was currently having was that the cold marriage she'd imagined she would escape turned out to be the one she was in, after all.

And the real trouble was that they'd had that wedding night. So now she knew. She *knew*.

Helene was certain that she could handle the rest of it. The tragedy was that her body had other ideas.

Even now, sobbing her eyes out and plotting foolish escapes from captivity, she could feel that insistent heat between her legs. That slickness that whispered dangerous things to her. That she should get up and try the door to the King's bedchamber. And upon discovering it locked, as she thought she would, why not head out into the hall and find a different way in? Or better yet, go outside, and see if she could make it along the wintry balcony that separated his room from hers?

She'd always thought that the best-case scenario would involve civility by day and a friendly, businesslike approach at night. She'd hoped that she wouldn't find whatever husband she ended up with physically repulsive, but even if she did, she'd hoped they could at least both behave with a certain amount of kindness. And everyone claimed that children were their own reward, so she was looking forward to that, too.

It had never occurred to her that she, born and raised to be a peacekeeper no matter her own feelings, could find herself in a situation like this.

Helene thought there must be something wrong with her, because all of her schooling had led her to believe that the most anyone could hope for when it came to marital relations was something pleasant. Perhaps gentle laughter might be involved, and a certain closeness.

Not this.

Not the enduring sensation that she'd been hollowed out by her own desire, left raw and unfinished, and possibly deformed by the things she wanted.

The good news was that it seemed as if Gianluca was so focused on what he believed to be her deception that he hadn't noticed.

Helene sighed a little bit and ran her hands over her hair. She had been trained to deal with her marriage. She would deal with her marriage, come what may.

But she wasn't her mother. She was not the sort of flower that could make do with any old soil and bloom prettily, on demand. Look what had already happened, and all she'd done was marry as expected.

She was going to have to choose a different sort of blooming altogether.

Helene turned that over, again and again, and

what she kept coming back to was the enduring ache inside her.

And the sure knowledge that no matter what Gianluca pretended now, he had been as bowled over by their night together as she had been. As she still was.

Maybe, she thought then, frowning at the cold glass and the world beyond, she was going about this all wrong.

Maybe it was time to stop playing his game and start playing her own.

"Besides," she murmured, her breath fogging against the windowpane, "it's not as if he can hate me *more,* is it?"

So she might as well try to get at least some of what she wanted out of this.

And maybe the prizes wouldn't be quite so stupid after all.

CHAPTER SEVEN

SOME WEEKS LATER, Gianluca found himself standing in the midst of another gala.

He couldn't have said what it was in aid of. He couldn't recall how many engagements he'd had this week. He'd forgotten everything his staff had whispered in his ear about the various dignitaries and such promenading about before him.

Because the only thing he could seem to concentrate on for any length of time was Helene.

Especially when they did events like this, where he could watch the way she charmed every person who crossed her path without even seeming to try.

"You look displeased, my king," she murmured through her serene smile when they took to the dance floor, always dancing for those few first moments before others joined them.

Though Gianluca never noticed the others.

"I am ruminating on your ability to hide the

fangs I know you carry," he said, but rather too late, because it was difficult not to get lost in all the ways she shone. "Right there behind that smile."

Helene did not look abashed. If anything, her smile grew brighter. "Fangs? How marvelous. Unless what you're telling me is that my dentistry needs work?"

Gianluca wanted to laugh, but controlled himself. Because he still couldn't believe that he had been taken in by the very sort of woman he had vowed to avoid. A woman like his own mother.

Women like Elettra, his father had told him on his deathbed, *hide in plain sight. A viper waiting to strike when you least expect it.*

Yet his viper made cracks about dentistry, right here in the middle of a ballroom, and what was he meant to do with that?

There was nothing to do, he knew, but dance.

As if this wasn't a game they played, but something real.

She had taken to her royal duties far too easily, he thought when the dancing was finished and they moved once more to the endless rounds of meeting and greeting the subjects who paid to attend galas like this for the chance to have a few moments of conversation.

So easily and so well, he couldn't help but

think as she dazzled the whole of the group before them, that it was tempting to ask himself what might have been. If she had been who she'd seemed to be on those summer walks in Provence.

He knew that was not a helpful line of thought.

But she acquitted herself beautifully at every engagement. She was charming, interesting, and the papers swooned daily not only over what they called the *royal romance* but the many ways their new queen epitomized all that a Fiammettan woman should be.

She was elegant. Poised. She was sophisticated enough to host a formal dinner consisting of heads of state and diplomats from afar, but down-to-earth enough to make everyone laugh, put everyone at ease, and make certain that no one at her table ever felt out of place.

And as many times as he told himself that it was that school she'd gone to, renowned as it was for turning out perfect hostesses just like this, Gianluca was well aware that there was something special about Helene.

Fangs, he told himself darkly as the night wore on. *Stuck deep beneath your ribs.*

It was no wonder he couldn't seem to catch a full breath in her presence.

Later, when he had given the expected speech

and they were sitting in the back of the car yet again, inching back toward the palace, she turned to him.

Gianluca expected barbs of some kind, no doubt involving those fangs she pretended she didn't know she had.

He braced himself, because it was only a matter of time. Now he'd made it clear that she wouldn't get her way, things between them would evolve the way his parents' relationship had. He expected that she would strike out at him, becoming more and more bitter by the day. The only upside was that he knew precisely where that led.

And precisely where he intended to put her, no matter how she sparkled in public.

But instead, Helene smiled at him.

In that pretty way of hers that made the gold in her eyes glow all the brighter, without the faintest hint of a fang in sight.

"It's going to be hard to act the broodmare if there's no breeding," she said.

And the shock of that went through him like an electric charge. "I beg your pardon?"

Gianluca couldn't have heard her right. He was sure he hadn't. He spent entirely too much time as it was replaying their wedding night on an endless loop in his head. And recalling those wild, hot hours filled him with a hard, edgy hunger that had him up and pacing, then trying to beat it out of himself in his workout room, to no avail.

But he knew women like this. He'd been raised by one. He had expected that once he'd uncovered her game, she would never indicate that she even knew what sex was unless she could use it against him. He'd expected her to dole it out, playing carrot and stick, and he'd assured himself that he would simply refuse to engage in her games.

This had to be a game—but he was too busy thinking about *breeding* with every last part of his instantly too-hot body to figure out what her goal was in playing it.

"My apologies," Helene said, in that particularly dry voice she used when she was being polite, but sharp.

Fang-sharp, he told himself.

"I keep forgetting that you are a king and perhaps don't muck about in the stables like some. You clearly don't understand how this works. If you want heirs, Gianluca, I'm afraid you will have to fight past your disgust for my deceitful ways and take me to your bed once again."

And there were so many things he could have said to that. He had the uncharacteristic urge to defend himself. To make it clear what it was he had distaste for and dampen whatever this was, because it couldn't be good—

But instead, it was as if his body took control of him. It was as if he became a different man.

Right there in the back of the royal limousine.

And he found he enjoyed it far more than he should have when her eyes widened. When her lips formed a perfect *oh* as he leaned toward her.

"We don't need a bed, *mia regina*," he growled at her. "I have told you this already, have I not? I always give my people what they want. Always."

And he proved it.

Then and there, while the motorcade made its way back up the hill to the royal palace.

When they got out of the car Helene was red-cheeked, her hair a mess, and yet she managed to march back to the royal apartments as if daring anyone to look at her sideways, with that elegance that was a part of her.

As if she was a true queen, something in him whispered.

And it was good to have that reminder, he told himself later—having restricted himself to his quarters, alone. Because he dared not take her twice again in one evening.

He already knew what that was like, and where it led.

Still, he assured himself as he stood in his

shower in the small hours of that same night, letting the cold water pound down upon him to no great effect, it was useful to remember that no matter how elegant she seemed at this gala or that function, no matter how sophisticated a queen she might appear, she was still a supposed virgin.

The one who had gone so wild on their wedding night that she'd made it clear she could not be any such thing, and then she'd gone ahead and compounded that error in the car tonight.

For he had tugged her to him, then into his lap.

And the moment they'd touched, it was as if they'd both been burned alive.

The flames *exploded* when he kissed her. When she kissed him back.

The conflagration grew between them, bigger, and yet bigger still—and after he helped himself to the long hem of that gown she wore, pushing the fabric up to her hips, he reached down to free himself and found her hands were already there.

"Mia regina," he had growled, and told himself it was a factual statement, that was all. *My queen.*

When she'd sunk herself down upon him, he had clenched his hands tight to grip her hips, because it was a process. She was so tight, so soft. And there was something mesmerizing about the way she fought to take the whole of his length.

Something almost unbearably hot.

It was when she'd managed to take all of him within her—shifting, bearing down, and then retreating to start again—that she let out a deep sort of sigh. She closed her eyes for a moment, as if *savoring him.*

Gianluca would never know how he had not lost control of himself entirely.

But she opened her eyes again. And then, holding his gaze as if she was the one who told the truth and always had—like a challenge—she had ridden them both to a mad, galloping finish.

He should not have second-guessed himself. She proved herself a liar every time they made contact. A wise man would not have been fooled a second time, no matter how excellent her training.

But his body didn't care if she told the truth or not, it only wanted more of her.

When the morning dawned, Gianluca redoubled his efforts to dig into her past. People never hid their sins as well as they imagined they did, so he knew he would uncover the real story about how she'd spent the past few years soon enough.

Yet in the meantime, he unlatched that door between their bedrooms and congratulated himself on persevering. Because, of course, he did this entirely for the bloodline.

Let her imagine he was the sort of man she could manipulate into abandoning his plans, if she liked. That changed nothing. She could brood about it up in his grandmother's retreat of stone and silence.

He was doing his duty, as he had always done. And as he would do again, when she bore him children and they were old enough to live without her.

"And what age is that, exactly, Gianluca?" Helene asked one night, in her mild way that he no longer quite believed. Because he could hear the edge beneath it now, that she hid beneath her lovely manners, and her cultured tones. "The age at which children are only too happy to live without their mothers?"

He had, for no reason at all, reiterated his precise plans for her. It had nothing to do with the fact that they had turned to each other when they walked into the royal apartments tonight, that he'd waved away his staff with a dismissive hand, or that he'd then carried her bodily to his bed. It had no relation to what followed from there, or to the fact that now they lay on the soft rug before the fire, both of them naked and gleaming with the force of their exertions.

All three times.

Helene sounded almost lazy as she asked him that question, and one thing he knew now about Helene was that she was in no way lazy.

"I was sent to boarding school when I was six years old," he said abruptly.

And he expected some sort of arch response, but all she did was prop herself up on one elbow. She raked the mess he'd made of her hair back from her face, then regarded him solemnly. "Six years old?"

Gianluca had the strangest urge toward defensiveness, then, when nothing could have made less sense to him. What did he have to be defensive about? He had been a crown prince, not a regular boy. Royal personages such as himself had been sent off to boarding school at young ages as long as boarding schools had existed.

"Some of my classmates began their education even earlier," he said, in freezing tones, and he would have sat up, perhaps removed himself from his conversation entirely, but he felt that would be more telling.

He did not want to tell her anything. Not about himself.

Especially not when a more layered version of the truth was that, despite his loneliness, he had often found school a reprieve from the dread and calamity of this palace. He had counted the days until he could return, no longer relegated to be as invisible as the furniture or a handy bit of cannon fodder.

Gianluca was appalled that he even *thought* such things. There was no possibility that he would *say* them. To anyone.

And certainly not her.

She was frowning at him as if what he said *hurt* her. "That doesn't sound like an education at all. It sounds like daycare. Or proper full-time care, I suppose."

"I'm deeply surprised by this attitude, Helene."

He did rise then. Gianluca stalked over to the bedside table, where he rang to have a light selection of food brought up, as he found himself famished.

It was no doubt his hunger that was affecting his mood.

When he was finished placing his order, he expected to find that Helene might have wrapped herself in something, but instead she stayed where she was.

Wholly naked, stretched out before the fire like every fantasy he had ever had, brought to vibrant and alluring life.

It was the lushness of her curves. It was the

dark waves of her hair that spilled all over her, dancing this way and that and making her more sensual every time she breathed. It was her eyes of melting brown and brilliant gold that made him—the King of Fiammetta, who bowed to no one—feel as if he was to prove himself to her.

Or for her, something in him whispered, but it was a voice he refused take on board.

He pretended he could not recognize it.

"You spent a great many years of your life in boarding school," he said, frowning at her because it was that or go to her again, to try once more to slake his unquenchable thirst for this woman. "And you credit your education for the ability to execute your duties as Queen in the way that you do. I would imagine you would exult in allowing your children to follow much the same path toward excellence."

He did not choose to recognize the way his pulse seemed to rush in him. He told himself it was a simple physical reaction, nothing more. Chemicals, that was all. Nothing he needed to consider any more closely than not—especially not when all he could see was that solemn gaze she aimed his way.

"I was sent to boarding school after my mother died," Helene said softly. But he was learning, too, that when her voice was soft, it did not make her weak. Or lessen the blow of anything she might be saying. And he did not like the fact that he knew such things. They made him wonder who she really was, this woman he had married under false pretenses that he still could not prove. "I was twelve. And all things considered, I would have preferred to have my mother."

"Children are not meant to stay forever with their parents," Gianluca gritted out, as if this was a fight he needed to win *right now.* As if this was about him instead of their hypothetical children.

"But they are expected stay for some while, surely. Or why bother having them at all? You could as easily adopt a few stray orphans off the street when they hit eighteen and they wouldn't know the difference."

Gianluca let out a deep sort of breath. "Your father is, at best, a minor noble. Mostly because of shrewd investments. By which I mean that you, though an heiress of gentle breeding, are not of noble blood."

"I don't recall ever claiming that my blood was blue." The look of something like a wicked amusement passed over her face, making the way she was lounging there seem to grab at him, until he was not at all certain that he was capable of keeping his distance. But he forced himself to stand fast. "I know you must have known this before you ever set eyes on me.

I've met every member of your staff by now, Gianluca. They are remarkably thorough."

He did not scowl. That would suggest a bigger reaction than he was having. "Bloodlines are of paramount importance when it is those very bloodlines that determine succession to a throne. Don't pretend you don't know this very well, please."

Helene sat up then and she took her time with it. She stretched like a cat and it was too much. It seemed to punch straight through his chest.

Like a knife, he told himself as he dug his palm against the sudden, searing ache.

The woman was a killer and he was letting her have her way.

But he did nothing as she got to her feet in that same, seemingly languid way she did everything, and then helped herself to one of the silk wrappers that his staff had taken to leaving in his rooms and hers now that there were no locked doors between them. Once she'd belted it and was covered in the finest silk, she drifted closer to him. He thought she might come to him, but instead she perched herself on the end of the bed, as if continuing a fascinating discussion.

When he was certain he had been trying to end it.

She looked entirely too serene. "Do you ever think about the fact that throughout all the ages past, no one could actually tell?"

"I do not know what you mean." Though he had an inkling.

"There are no paternity tests. There were just...regular people storming about, pretending their feelings were facts. On some level, how can you possibly know what your bloodline is or isn't?"

"Is this how you think you will convince me of your innocence?" he asked, his voice barely above a whisper.

And most people would cringe at that. Bow their heads in shame, at the very least.

But all Helene did was shrug.

Insolently.

"I think it's the guilty who run around trying to get others to buy their story." And if anything, if possible, she looked even *more* at ease. "I feel no need to prove my innocence. I know it to be true. I'm the one who's lived every day of my life, after all. I would know if I had accidentally collected a selection of lovers, but then again, so too would your staff. Funnily enough, I think they've come up empty-handed too. Why do you think that is?"

And he could have raged about her offhandedness. He could have made certain she knew that he wasn't giving up and that he was in fact tracking down every stray lead. He could have put his mouth on hers and quelled her insolence at the source—

But instead, there was a faint knock on the door that indicated the arrival of the food he'd ordered.

Gianluca told himself that was a relief.

Just as he told himself that he was not succumbing to temptation, but merely making certain that he had as many opportunities as possible to get her pregnant as quickly as he could, so this torture might end.

That was why she fell asleep in his bed that night, the way she had been doing with some regularity by now. Even though it was something he'd vowed to himself he would never allow again.

Over the following days, he reviewed his staff's findings, not best pleased to find that she was right. They had found nothing. Everything she said about her past was easily verifiable. If she was hiding something, it was so well hidden only she knew about it.

"And of course, sire," his personal aide said in a tone stripped of even the faintest hint of any inflection, "a secret is only really a secret if no one else knows it. And if that's the case here, it's unlikely that it's a secret anyone else could tell. Which is a victory, is it not?"

For he had told them that he wanted to make

certain no one could ever step forward with any so-called secrets from the Queen's past. He'd intimated that there might have been some cause for worry, so that they would look harder.

Instead he was left with something far worse than any confirmation of the sins he knew she'd committed.

And that was his urge to believe her.

But he knew better.

To underscore that some days later—or to remind himself of what was truly at stake here—he gritted his teeth and took his least favorite walk of all. He had watched his queen charm the better part of Europe. He had proven himself unable to keep any promise to himself when it came to erecting boundaries between them. He was disastrously close to becoming a version of his father, and that could not stand.

And so he took himself out one of the small, hidden doors at the rear of the palace. He crossed the wintry grounds, winding his way through the ancient cottages and chapels and ruins of old castles until he could present himself to the guards who stood before the farthest cottage, closest to the stables without actually being a part of them.

It was a bitterly cold February day. Sullen snow fell insistently from low, gray clouds, with winds from the tops of the surrounding mountains sharp enough to draw blood.

Adequate preparation for an interaction with Elettra, to his mind.

He nodded to the guards and was instantly admitted, and though he immediately wished he had not come at all, he walked through to get this done.

"To what do I owe this unimaginable honor, Your Majesty?" asked his mother as she rose from the seat where she waited for him in her lovely drawing room, sketching a perfectly appropriate curtsy that still somehow managed to scrape at him, as if she was mocking him. "When your secretary called and ordered me to clear the afternoon, I could hardly believe my ears. The King of Fiammetta? Polluting the very shades of the dower house?"

Gianluca ignored all that. He would ignore his mother entirely if he could, and he usually did, but he had come here to speak to her. Ignoring her would be a waste of time.

He looked around this room that he had entered only a handful of times before. If he remembered right, while his grandmother had still been alive. And though the furnishings were very much the same, they were brighter than he recalled. Happier.

As if his mother liked to let in the light, when there was light to let in.

He didn't like how that sat in him, like a hint he ought to take.

Just as he didn't like the fact that most of the pictures on her mantel were not of her with various celebrities, as one would expect from such a dedicated attention-seeker as Elettra.

Instead, they were all of him.

There was even the official wedding photo that had been released worldwide, showing Gianluca and Helene gazing at each other as they exited the cathedral. He did not wish to investigate why it was he didn't like that picture here, either.

"I did not come here to fence words with you, Madam," he told her with as much formality as he could muster.

Elettra sighed as if he'd said something provocative, then sank back down on the nearest settee, where she set about pouring out hot cups of tea. When Gianluca was certain she must remember he could not abide the stuff.

"Afternoon tea is not, strictly speaking, a Fiammettan ritual, though we have adopted it," his mother told him, and he felt some great storm inside him, though he refused to acknowledge it.

He wanted no part of it, but there was something about her voice. Gianluca had the strangest memory then that he rejected almost at once, certain it was far more likely to be an invention of that six-year-old child who had cried himself to sleep every night in that school where he'd been sent. Something he had never admitted to another living soul.

Gianluca had learned to tell himself that he was merely imagining things. That he had no memories of his childhood. That his mother had certainly never gathered him onto her lap, and read to him.

That she had never told him stories or taken his little hand in hers to walk with him around the palace, telling him made-up names for things that he absolutely did not remember today, damn it.

She was still going on about tea. "It was when one of your great-grandfathers procured himself an Englishwoman for a queen. She brought the wonderful tradition of afternoon tea in the British style with her when she came here, and so there have been Fiammettan tea shops ever since. Do you not remember? I used to take you there—"

"I have always hated tea," he told her, sternly.

But Elettra did not seem dismayed. She merely set down a teacup in his direction, then sat back with her own and sipped at it.

It made him want to shout, though he restrained himself.

"And here I thought you wanted to meet with me so we could debate, once again, whether we prefer scones or crumpets," she murmured.

He wanted to dismiss that as a kind of foolishness too, but Gianluca found that it hit him strangely. His mouth almost watered. He could almost taste the scones he loved so much, though he did not associate them with his mother. Still, it was true that he indulged himself from time to time, in the privacy of his own quarters.

"How many lovers did you take when you were married to my father, the late King?" he asked icily instead.

And his reward, such as it was, was the slight widening in his mother's eyes, dark like his. She set her teacup down in the saucer she held with a click, then placed them both on the table before her. He thought that it took her a moment or so to raise her gaze to his, but when she did, her expression was smooth and unreadable, the way it always was.

"I wonder," Elettra said quietly, "what would become of us, you and I, if just once we stopped playing these games." He said nothing, and her lips curved into something sad. "If you and I stopped having arguments with people who are no longer in the room."

"Is it an argument?" He watched her closely. "Or is it that I find myself wondering, from time to time, if I have been less merciful with you than I should. If perhaps I should look to my benevolence in my dealings with you and revise my impressions. So I ask again, how many lovers did you take? And of them, how many did you leak to the press yourself?"

Elettra folded her hands in her lap and sat there with a dignity that enraged him, as certainly she did not deserve it. Surely her own sins should have precluded her from even the faintest shred of dignity, assumed or otherwise.

Yet somehow, without changing her expression, she managed to make it clear that he had disappointed her once again.

Gianluca did not sit taller, as he had half a mind to do at that—some deep-seated vestige of the child he must once have been. Instead, he relaxed as he stood, and leaned against the mantel, his back to all those pictures of himself through the ages.

"Come now. You had so much to say in all of those interviews, one after the next, each one a nail in the coffin not only of your marriage, but of our people's trust in their leaders." He shook his head. "Not once did it occur to you that you were leaving me to clean up after you. A king in name only, because in truth I am a janitor, forever trailing after you and attempting to make your trash disappear."

Elettra's eyes flashed. "How poetic, darling," she said. "I didn't know you had it in you."

And yet he felt as if something was lost when all she did was pick up her tea once more.

"I must thank you." He straightened from the mantel and affected his own bow, deep enough to be mocking. "You are, as ever, precisely as I expected you to be."

"You're so discerning," his mother murmured, as if in agreement. "And in no way afflicted by confirmation bias, my son and king."

"I'm certain you've cast yourself the victim of your own crimes," he said, but he was already heading for the door. "Thank you for reminding me why I keep you separate from everything that matters."

It was good that he'd come here. She was his past, but also his future if he did not handle this terrible attraction to his own queen, herself a proven liar as well.

He hated that he'd needed the reminder.

And he told himself that he was dismissing her once again as he pushed his way back outside into a day gone grayer, colder.

But he heard her parting shot anyway.

And with that laugh of hers that made it all the more damaging, hitting him right between the shoulder blades.

"Because, of course, the King of Fiammetta could never be wrong. By definition. Just like your father, is that not so?"

CHAPTER EIGHT

FAITH MESSAGED ONE MORNING, some two months into Helene's marriage.

Why did I have to read about the fact that you met my most favorite singer in all the world in a tabloid magazine?

Then she devolved into shouting by text.

YOU KNOW HOW MUCH I LOVE HIM!

Helene dutifully texted back a full play-by-play of her interaction with the singer in question, and even indulged in the sort of silly, make-believe gossip she and her cousin had enjoyed in the past. Where they made up a wild speculation about people they would never meet, and then treated it as fact. Helene thought that was the least she could do, having actually met the man.

While she left her cousin satisfied that Faith, and Faith alone, was the one true love of a rather odd young man she was unlikely to ever meet, the exchange left Helene unsettled.

The feeling followed her through a day of her usual duties. A morning of classes and correspondence, because it was her office that was responsible for sending out cards for all manner of occasions to the Fiammettan subjects. And because it offered her a way to ask her aides about all kinds of subjects that interested her after, like the previous king and queen. And the day's headlines, chock-full of palace intrigue.

She wrote cards, asked questions, and listened not only to what her staff said—but what they didn't.

"My mother always said that any man must know trouble, whether in a crown or in a quarry," one of her aides said in German after one of Helene's leading questions about Gianluca's parents.

"Heavy is the head," another replied in French, with significant looks all around.

This was standard. They would deny if asked—Helene had tried—but none of her staff cared for the former king. And they were all of them staunch royalists, or they wouldn't be here, tending to her.

She tucked that away with all of the other details that she hoped she could weave into some kind of tapestry that, one day, she could look at and make sense of her husband at last.

Every day she got a little closer. She was sure of it.

But for some reason, over the last ten days or so, she'd begun to find all of it, all the waiting and weaving…exhausting.

And today when she was free, instead of taking her usual walk in the palace gardens—which she did no matter what the weather or Gianluca's desire for photo opportunities, though those were fewer now that they were seen together so often at events—Helene headed down to her favorite library instead.

Outside there was another snowstorm brewing, this one extreme enough that even the natives had raised a brow or two in concern. Helene sat by the fire, and for once, didn't find herself a few books to read. Not today. Somehow, she wasn't quite in the mood.

Instead, she found herself gazing into the fire, and trying to reason through why it was that a perfectly normal exchange with her cousin this morning had left her feeling so…bereft.

And the answer didn't take long, but still, it seemed a bit longer than it should have. The way everything did lately.

She was stuck in a gloomy marriage she

couldn't escape if she wanted to, so that giggling about make-believe relationships her cousin wasn't having seemed like a reprieve.

Though even as she thought that, she knew that the true problem with her marriage was that it wasn't *gloomy* at all.

On the contrary.

Everything with Gianluca was white hot and *wild*.

And to her astonishment, there was no getting used to him. There was no reaching a saturation point. Every time he touched her it was better than the time before. Every time they came together, no matter where they came together, it was as if it was the first time. And the last time.

It was that epic. It was that unbearably beautiful.

It was that catastrophic.

Because the truth was, Helene thought as she watched the dancing flames of the fire before her, she really did want those fairy tales. The ones her mother had told her when she was a girl. The ones she and Faith created for each other about pop singers who fancied themselves ambassadors to the world, and anyone else who took their fancy. She wanted all those stories. She wanted to be an old woman who could look wisely at young girls like the ones at her luncheon today and tell them that it was all worth waiting for, whatever perfect fairy tale they carried within them, because it would happen.

If they believed. And if they let it come.

And sometimes *letting it come* took too long, so a woman did what she needed to do to prod a man along.

It wasn't that she defied Gianluca. Not outwardly.

But she used the weapons she had.

Without mercy.

She had to believe that if she could only show him how, he might come around to her way of seeing things. And that maybe if she showed him who she really was, in bed and out, he would finally believe her.

And maybe then she would get to see that smile of his again.

That practical girl inside her, who had thought she could march into a frigid marriage with a total stranger only to fall in love at first sight, wasn't so sure. Because she might believe in fairy tales, but now she knew too well that even when something seemed to be moving in that direction, it could turn out to hinge entirely on an innocence she could not prove. And that he would not believe.

No matter how many times he called her *mia regina* and made her sob out his name in reply.

"In other words," she muttered into the fire, "you're doomed."

Helene woke sometime later, surprised to find she'd drifted off into a very uncharacteristic nap. But there was no time to worry over it, because while she and Gianluca had no outside engagements tonight, her aides had come to ready her for one of their private dinners in their palace apartments. The dinners Gianluca insisted on, because, she thought, it made him imagine they were more civilized than they were afterward, in his bed. Or hers. Or wherever they found themselves in a set of apartments with so very many rooms.

And though she might think differently in the aftermath, Helene could find nothing *gloomy* about spending time with her husband.

It was the way Gianluca waited for her each evening. He stood there looking resplendent as always, even though their private dinners were meant to be casual. He usually wore only a shirt and trousers, while she liked her jeans and something pretty on top.

But there was never any doubt that he was the King, no matter what he wore.

Or didn't.

He was there before the windows, so that the lights of this beautiful kingdom glittered behind him through the storm. Sometimes she thought she saw the same lights in his dark night gaze, the way they'd been there that first night.

Before everything changed.

And maybe that unexpected nap still had its claws in her, because her usual jolting reaction to the sight of him didn't seem to translate into the lightheartedness she liked to use at dinners like this. If only to confound him.

It hadn't occurred to her that *not* doing it would confound him too.

Halfway through the meal he sat back in his seat and eyed her even more closely than usual. "Are you unwell?"

"Not to my knowledge," she replied, frowning at him. "Why?"

He studied her frown, making Helene wonder if she'd never actually *frowned* at him before now. Surely not.

"You do not seem your normal self."

And this was clearly true, because she shot back, "I didn't realize you knew what that was, Gianluca."

And she expected him to glower, but to her surprise, he tipped his wineglass in her direction. "Fair enough."

And Helene felt…listless and yet half frenzied, all at once. She had the urge to leap up from her chair and *do something*. Dance down the length of the table, for example, kicking the fine china to and fro and watching it shatter. Whatever it took to break all these unspoken rules they followed these days.

That they would have these excruciatingly civilized dinners, then tear each other apart after dessert. But never, ever, both at once.

It was always the same sequence of events and while it was true that they knew each other intimately, in ways she hadn't known one person could know another, what did it mean? She knew the precise shape of that tender place between his ear and the sideburn he kept trimmed short, and how it fit her fingertip when she stroked him there. She knew the entire vocabulary of his moans and groans and how to make them into a kind of song as she took her time with him. She knew his scents, his tastes, and the shape their bodies made together when they were both asleep.

And she knew every thread of the tapestry she was building, every color and weight of each story she read or heard, all leading her closer to him. Everyone she encountered added to it. Everyone they met contributed a tale about his parents or him, and she thought that really, she was the reigning expert on King Gianluca.

Save him.

But he wouldn't discuss it.

And tonight she was tired of quietly weaving.

"Tell me," she demanded without any preamble, "one happy memory from your childhood. Can you do that?"

"Do I appear to you to be riddled with childhood wounds, Helene?"

And on another night she might have made an elegant sort of demurral and waved that away. Tonight she only sat back in her chair, held his gaze, and raised a challenging brow instead.

Because she knew the answer—that there was not one part of him that childhood hadn't touched, warped, even ruined—but she also knew he would likely get up and leave if she shared her learned opinion that he was, in fact, a *walking* wound from the things that had happened to him during his childhood.

He let out one of those laughs of his, short and sharp, more a surprised bark than anything else. And she rather thought that he would storm off, though he hadn't done that in some while… but he didn't.

Instead, he looked at her as if he was trying to see beneath her skin, and she became aware of too many things all at once.

That everything was *different* tonight, or she was. She could feel too much, as if the Vivaldi that played gently in the background was winding its way in and around her body instead of simply filling the air.

And she felt *desperate* straight through, when that was the most absurd feeling of all. She was a queen. Sitting in a king's private dining room, in the palace they shared, eating another feast prepared by the finest chefs in all of Europe, according to her husband. She was listening to classical music while making awkward, yet polite, conversation about charity events and current issues.

There was nothing *desperate* about this.

So maybe it was her.

"My father was always quite busy with matters of state, appropriately," Gianluca said into the messiness swirling around inside her, and even though moments before—seconds before—Helene had wanted to kick off her shoes and dance on the tabletop, she was suddenly riveted by him. Gazing at him, just there on the other side of this corner of the long table they shared, as if she had no intention of ever looking away again. "I was left in the care of tutors and nannies and the like. But at night, a woman would come into the nursery, take me in her lap, and read me a nighttime story. Every story was…a different world. I suppose even a prince in a castle liked the idea of imagining himself somewhere else."

He looked very nearly defensive then, and she felt almost breathless, as if the slightest move on her part would ruin everything and break whatever fragile thread this was between them, suddenly.

Because, for once, Gianluca did not look serious or betrayed. For a moment, she could almost see the little boy he must have been. Before they'd sent him away from here to whatever dire boarding school took in six-year-olds. When that smile she might not have seen too often, but could recall perfectly, wasn't so rare.

"My mother used to read to me too," she said.

But it was the wrong thing to say. She could see it in the way his brows drew together. "I didn't say it was my mother."

She blinked. "You said it was a woman, and it sounded as if it wasn't a nanny or a tutor...?"

"I have long since left escapist fiction behind, I'm afraid." He sounded curt. Dark. "That's what happens as a person grows up. There's no time for such stories when there are so many real-world things to consider instead."

"I don't think you could say anything I would disagree with more." But she smiled a little as she said it, because she knew, somehow, that he was remarkably vulnerable just now. She just knew. "I think that human beings need stories. We need to engage our imagination or we are doomed to lose ourselves."

"In what? Reality?" He shook his head. "That is not doom. That is life."

"But if you can't imagine yourself out of a bad reality, what will become of you?" she countered. "And what better way to train for that than reading stories?"

"Is your reality so heinous, Helene?"

She could see that he hadn't moved, not even a millimeter, and yet she felt as if he had. As if he'd stood up, then loomed over her, crowding into her space and taking over her senses.

"I didn't say it was. That doesn't change how I feel about the necessity of stories, Gianluca. Fairy tales teach people how to *be* people."

"Some stories are necessary," he gritted out, as if they were in a desperate fight that he needed to win. "The story of the Kingdom, that all its subjects can share in. These specific beliefs we all must live by to do so in relative peace with the hope of prosperity. But you are speaking of something else. When surely you should know that the purpose of such tales was never singing seafood and dancing candelabras. The first fairy tales were no doubt told over the fires of yore as morality tales. Warnings, not love stories. Making them something else not only takes their power, it steals your own."

"Or," Helene returned with precious little

hold on her hard-won charm, "they are just good stories, no matter what you use them for."

"At heart, they are lies." Gianluca's voice was harsh and unequivocal. "And I cannot abide lies."

"What sort of lies do you mean?" she asked softly, carefully, because she had woven that tapestry so carefully and so steadily and now she was tugging on its threads. And she couldn't seem to stop, not now that she could see a glimpse of the real Gianluca shining through. Not even though she knew that she was risking everything here. And worse, risking hurting him in the process. "Like the one where you pretend that the only happy memory you can draw up from your childhood involves a random servant? I think both you and I know that's not the case."

"Damn you," he growled at her.

And then he really did rise from his chair. And he really was looming over hers, with a look on his face that she'd never seen before.

As if the ice she'd cracked was him.

Then Gianluca was hauling her up, slamming his mouth to hers, and breaking all of his own rules.

She half expected him to shove all the china out of his way, onto the hard floor, but he was still Gianluca. He lifted her up into his arms, dragging her thighs around his waist, and carried her down to the far end of the table, where the table was not covered in dishes and he could lay her out like a feast.

And then he proceeded to eat her alive.

And it was different this time. There was something *different*, as if both of them were naked in ways they never had been before. As if they were both too raw to do anything but show themselves, and Helene couldn't understand that entirely, but everything in her was open to this, whatever it was.

To him, however he came to her.

Especially when it was as if they had revealed themselves tonight in ways so new there was nothing to do but imprint on each other with every touch. With every hard, deep kiss. With the way he dug his hands into her hair, then tipped back her face as if he could make a whole meal out of her mouth alone.

He really did try, and Helene tried back.

But it didn't last, because every time they built a fire, a new one raged, and they seemed unable to do anything but throw gas on each.

Her hands were busy and shaky at his waist. She ripped his shirt off, heedless of the buttons that popped off and hit the floor. Because it was necessary, more necessary than breath, to put her mouth on the glory of his bare chest and then to trace with her hands that arrow of dark hair that led her right where she wanted to go.

He didn't let her get there. Not this time. He muttered something she didn't understand, though it seemed to fill her all the same.

Then his hands were at the hem of her shirt, pulling it up and off. He made a low noise of deep male approval at the site of the frilly, lacy thing she wore beneath, but then he pushed it up and out of his way. Then he took that off of her too.

Gianluca drew one proud nipple into his mouth, making another low sort of noise when she arched into him, giving him better access. And delivering herself directly into the carnal delight of that hot, clever mouth of his.

Helene could do nothing, then, but surrender. As he went on and on, teasing her and taunting her, until she was begging him. Pleading with him.

Until he bent her back against the table, slid his hand down beneath her waistband, and palmed her wet heat at last.

Then he played her like some kind of classical instrument, making her a part of the symphony that soared all around them, as he slowly, expertly, tore her apart.

Once. Then again.

And then, while she shook and sobbed,

Gianluca pulled the rest of her clothes off. He kicked off his own, and then, with a glorious ferocity, slammed his way into her.

He folded up her legs between them so she was wide open, completely his. No barriers, no control, nothing but the way he thrust deep, again and again.

Helene opened her eyes, gripping his shoulders as he braced himself above her. She held his gaze as he slammed into her and made her bloom with each thrust, shoving the heavy, antique table across the floor.

It should have been a kind of madness, but it was something else.

Because his eyes were on hers and she could see those stars again.

And Helene knew she wasn't the only one who understood that there was something profound in this moment. That despite themselves, they had moved into a different place.

That this was the kind of prize she had only hoped she'd find when she'd decided that she wouldn't hide from him. When she'd decided that she would fight for the both of them whether he wanted to help her or not.

This was what she won—the glory of it built high—and she hurtled over the edge once more. And when she floated back again, he was still inside her, huge and hard.

But this time, he lowered himself against her, drawing her legs around his waist.

And then, keeping that gaze of his locked on hers, Gianluca went slow.

Time spun out and lost all meaning.

Helene clung to him, but even as she did, she felt as if she was inside him as he was inside her. As if they were both a part of the same thing, wrapped up tight like this. Made new every time he found himself inside her.

Sanctified here, together.

Something broke over her that wasn't another shattering, not yet. Helene shifted, reaching up to cup his dark, stern face between her palms. And he looked even more austere now, the stark lines of desire making him seem something like cruel, when she knew he wasn't. Not really.

No matter how he liked to pretend, because there was this.

A cruel man could not make love.

Maybe this was the truth she'd been looking for all along, because it settled in her now like sunlight. As if it was a fact she had always known.

"Your problem," she whispered, because there were other things she knew, "is that deep down, you trusted me all along."

She watched her words wash over him, then through him. And then become a part of that same pure sunlight as he roared out his release, flooding her and sending her catapulting over that edge once more.

Into nothing but the brightest light.

And for a long time after that, neither one of them could move.

When he did, he pulled her up so she was sitting there with her legs dangling off the table, dazed.

But, something in her whispered, *defiant, too.*

Maybe that was what the truth did. Or better still, speaking it out loud.

Gianluca gazed down at her, his face stern.

"I wish I could believe you," he told her, his voice gravelly. Rough. "Just as I wish I could believe those fairy stories my mother read me." He reached over to trace the line of her lips with his thumb, as if he couldn't help himself. Yet in those night sky eyes of his, Helene saw only dark. "But I don't."

And she was both unsurprised and deeply shocked that he walked away and left her there.

She put her clothes back on, carefully, as if she was hurt when she wasn't. Maybe she wished she was, as then she might have something to tend to. Instead she set the dining room to rights and only then, having hidden the evidence from any staff members who hadn't heard the table moving, did she wander out.

Then make her way back to her own bedroom, where she curled herself up in a ball and wished that she could cry.

Instead, she lay awake until late, wishing she didn't feel as if all the skin had been flayed from her bones.

And the next morning she woke up to Faith's monthly complaints about how wretched she felt, because she and Helene usually felt the same sort of wretched at the same time. She started typing back—

Then stopped.

Helene sat straight up in her bed, and even though she hadn't slept well, too caught up in dark eyes filled with stars, then not, and all the things they hadn't said that had flowed between them last night and left her *flayed* and *raw*, she was filled with a wild energy.

A certainty, more like.

She scrolled through the calendar on her phone. She started counting back on her fingers, to double-check.

But she already knew.

She thought of her listlessness. How outside her own skin she felt. How raw she was lately. How incapable of the simplest things, when she'd used to pride herself in taking refuge in perfect dinner table conversation.

It was no fairy tale that she had been here two

months and had been both having sex and doing nothing to protect herself from its consequences that whole time. She hadn't had a period since some two weeks before her wedding.

That was truth. That was reality.

And she knew.

Helene sat there on the high bed, her hands over the belly she'd never really given much thought to before. Did she already feel some kind of thickening? She'd thought that was simply all the rich food she ate now that there was no wedding gown to model for half the world…

But it wasn't the food.

Helene was pregnant.

She was *pregnant.*

And it was as if a kind of floodgate burst open, then.

Because once she accepted what a missed period indicated, when she had never missed a period in her life, it was as if everything else fell into place.

She felt kind of wild clarity that she'd never felt before.

And there was a peace in it, too.

Because there was absolutely no way in hell that she was letting her child grow up like this.

There would be no boarding schools at six years old.

There would be no chilly parents, tearing strips off of each other for the child to hear.

She had loved her mother, she would always love her mother, but Helene had no desire whatsoever to *become* her. And she knew, because she'd tried.

While it was always possible that her parents had a different relationship behind closed doors, Helene had no intention of showing her children weakness or acceptance in the face of cruelty.

And she had no intention of becoming *his* parents, either.

She would not raise a child who would pretend not to remember whether or not his own mother had read them stories.

Her children would not grow up the way that he had. Or the way that she had, either.

Gianluca had been right when he'd said that she was not of the sort of aristocratic blood that he was. Her people had fought across the ages for every scrap of what they had. They had not had palaces to retreat into or armies to carry their banners. They had done it all themselves.

And she, Helene Archibald San Felice, the Queen of Fiammetta, would do no less.

Starting now.

CHAPTER NINE

AT FIRST GIANLUCA thought that Helene was having the same sort of hangover that he was after that night. When things had become entirely too raw between them, in ways he wasn't sure he wanted to analyze.

Nor could.

On the surface they carried on as they had been. They had a full roster of royal engagements and neither one of them was the sort to scrimp on such things. He might not trust her, as he had said. But he did know her to be a hard worker in that sense.

Is that the character of a liar? came that voice again, and again he ignored it.

Tonight they were at yet another formal event. And Gianluca, who prided himself on knowing as many details as possible about everything that went on in his kingdom, in his name, and with all the charities that he spearheaded, had completely forgotten what this event was even *for*.

He was beginning to wonder if he had over-committed to this charity circuit of his, all of it calculated to prove to his people that he was a far better king than his father had ever been.

That his reign would be filled only with positive things, and as few negative things as possible.

But it had been easier to focus on such things when he wasn't married. When there wasn't Helene.

Because liar or not, he would far rather spend an evening with her, alone.

She told him happy little stories of her time in that boarding school she'd gone to, making the whole thing sound like a sparkling adventure when he knew full well it was one of the most restrictive schools in existence. She told him stories about her late mother and growing up in that château in Provence, where, in her telling, it was always a sunny day in summer and even Herbert was an entertaining character, in his way.

Gianluca even liked it when she argued with him, in that understated way she had. As if, could she only prod him gently enough, he would realize the error of his ways and happily see her side of things.

And she did it all so adroitly that sometimes, he almost did.

But his father had taught him well what liars women were. And how could he have believed otherwise when a man so grand, so captivated by his own magnificence, had declared such things? Had shouted them? Had overturned tables as punctuation?

Something in him hitched at that memory, but he shoved it aside with the ease of long practice.

Women lied. Especially when they claimed otherwise. And though Helene had fooled him well—she had revealed herself on their wedding night. Much as he might wish that she hadn't. Much as, some nights, he lay with her curled around him and wished he could forget it.

The truth was the truth whether he liked it or not.

Because if it wasn't, then he would not need to watch himself so carefully when he was around her. He would not have to fight so hard to contain this wild addiction to her. To let it out only when they were alone and he could make sure not to say anything he would regret, by filling his mouth with her instead.

These were all things he would prefer to do back at the palace, he admitted tonight. Instead of having been dragged into some tedious conversation with other world leaders that had nothing to do with governing and everything to do with the photo opportunity.

Gianluca was sick unto his soul of *photo opportunities* in place of reality.

Though he did not intend to delve into why that was. Not tonight.

He looked for his queen instead.

As ever, Helene was not hard to find. She was too bright, too astonishingly lush, in a sea of Afghan hound sameness. There were a great many glittering jewels on a great many aristocratic necks in this elaborate mountainside venue tonight, but there was only one gleaming queen.

And she was his.

Gianluca was so enchanted by her, the way he did not like to admit he always was, that it took him a long moment to recognize the woman she was speaking to. The two of them stood close together over by a set of the voluptuous orchids that were serving as the better part of the decor for this gala.

He had to blink to be certain, but there was no mistake. Helene was deep in conversation with none other than the Lady Lorenza, his father's infamous first lover.

There was no reason for a chill to go through him, as if he was looking at some kind of ghost.

No reason at all, and yet he started moving through the crowd at once, hardly noticing how easily it parted before him. And as he moved, he accepted the unpalatable truth that Helene was the only person he had ever encountered who made him feel that he was some kind of a fool.

It was always something.

There was always some hint that she was out-maneuvering him when that should have been impossible. He was the King of Fiammetta and she was a sheltered girl who'd been raised to marry a rich man. To contribute her lovely genes to a set of predetermined bloodlines, and no, he did not care to think too closely about the comments she'd made about the provenance of those bloodlines.

As he moved across the gala floor, Gianluca entertained the possibility that Helene really was that girl, bright and sparkling perhaps, but without the ulterior motives. That girl might very well have found herself speaking to the Lady Lorenza who, despite her past with King Alvize, had ever since lived an entirely blame-less life. Gianluca had seen her earlier in the evening, here at the charity gala with her own son—who despite much speculation in the press, bore an unmistakable resemblance to her husband and not to the former king. And there were a thousand reasons why the Queen of Fi-ammetta might speak to one of the Kingdom's aristocrats.

But, somehow, Gianluca knew none of those were Helene's reason tonight. Not only because he knew that she was not as naïve as she might pretend. That even if he had somehow misread the situation on his wedding night—an impossibility—there was the fact that the girls who came out of the Institut were taught how to function as weapons, not merely wives.

It was why he'd asked to meet her in the first place.

More fool you, he thought darkly.

He closed the distance between him and his wife and as he did, it was Lady Lorenza who saw him coming. And in so doing, confirmed what Gianluca already thought, by putting up her hand as if to stop whatever Helene was saying to her.

When Helene looked over her shoulder to see him there, Gianluca thought she should have looked guilty. With her sins all over her face, for once.

Instead, the look on her face was rather more speculative. Gianluca did not like it.

He found himself perilously close to a scowl, right here in public, but caught himself at the last moment and merely took Helene's arm.

Then inclined his head toward Lady Lorenza as she curtsied before him.

"It is a pleasure to see you, as always," he said, with great formality.

"It is an honor, Your Majesty," she replied, with her usual faultless manners.

It all made his jaw hurt, this sharp game of courtesy, and he ordered himself to unclench it. There was nothing objectionable about this woman, he told himself, not for the first time. She could not be blamed for having dated the young King Alvize. But Gianluca also knew that every second he spent in her presence led to tabloid whispers, unsubstantiated rumors, and a resurgence of all the old nonsense he liked to think dead and buried.

And suddenly he had the strangest memory. Of being all of seventeen and at a party a great deal like this one. He had come across Lorenza there, and they had talked politely, about nothing in particular that he could recall. Had she not been *the infamous Lady Lorenza*, he doubted he would have remembered the interaction at all.

But *Like father like son!* the tabloids had blared.

Gianluca might have laughed the whole thing off, so absurd was the very notion that anything untoward might ever have happened between them—much less when he was a teenager—but his father had gone into a terrifying black rage.

He didn't like to think about the things that had happened then. The things his father had said. And done.

And worse, threatened to do.

Gianluca avoided Lorenza as much as possible without being impolite, even though his father had been dead a decade.

He made his excuses now as he steered Helene away from her.

"That was rude." Helene's voice was very pleasant and pitched so that only he could hear what she said. Anyone else would take it for far happier conversation. "She and I were speaking."

"You and she have nothing to speak about."

"All anyone ever talks about when it comes to Lady Lorenza is your father. Did you know that she's actually an incredibly interesting woman in her own right?"

"I cannot imagine that you're going to tell me anything I don't already know. But what I can tell you, what you should know above all else, is that this is not a topic I wish to discuss. Ever."

Helene carried on as if she hadn't heard him. "After she finished with your father, she went to school. Back to school. Whereupon she got numerous degrees in anthropology and now spends her time either on digs or at the offices of the University of Fiammetta, where she is also a professor. Her son has followed in her footsteps, and though he teaches at a rival university, they have managed to fund a fair few digs together. Her daughter teaches literature at one of the colleges here in the city. They are a very brainy, learned, academic family, including her husband, who has something of a mad scientist bent and, while not swanning about being an aristocrat, invents things in his spare time."

Gianluca could not stop dead in the middle of the floor the way he would have liked to do. That would give all the gossips something else to chew upon, and they would. With relish. So instead, he pulled her along with him until he could steer her outside, where braziers had been set out in the renovated castle's courtyard to cut the chill of the winter night. Once there, his guards quickly cleared the space of the inevitable trysts and smokers so that he and the Queen could have a moment alone.

He hoped this would seem romantic to the audience watching them from within.

And to help with that, he turned his back to the glass doors and windows so anyone gawking would see only Helene. "I cannot imagine what makes you think I wish to know the details about that woman's family. Or anything else concerning her." He bit that out, not sure he liked his words any better when he could see them puff in the air before him. But that didn't make them any less true. "The Lady Lorenza is not an appropriate person for you to be seen talking to, Helen. Surely you must know this."

"She didn't do anything wrong." Helene's gaze seemed particularly intense, there beneath the glow of the artificial heat, and he found himself moving closer to her. To block her from anyone watching, he assured himself. That was all. "Do you know why she broke things off with your father?"

Gianluca did not understand why she was continuing with this line of discussion when he had made it clear that it displeased him. "She has always stated that she found the media coverage entirely too intense."

"I'm sure that's part of it. There's no denying that it's all a bit mad. The paparazzi can take the most intrusive pictures, then say anything they like, and there's no recourse." Helene frowned, suddenly. "Just yesterday I read an unhinged story about us. You apparently have a secret mistress stashed away on the palace grounds who you visit in secret, right under my nose. You are your father, naturally, and I am being cast as prudish yet also angelic, as if they haven't quite worked out what character I'll be playing."

He did nothing to control his scowl then.

"You shouldn't be reading that trash. It's forbidden in the palace for a reason."

"I hate to break this to you, Gianluca, but there is such a thing as the internet." She shrugged as if she didn't see the look on his face. "Besides, my cousin Faith and I have an ongoing competition to see which one of us can find the most outrageous tabloid article about me. Some days, it's a draw. But my point is, that's not why Lady Lorenza broke up with your father."

Gianluca couldn't navigate the shifts in this conversation. He couldn't—or he didn't want to. He wasn't certain there was a difference.

He felt, again, that he was out of his depth. He, who had only yesterday navigated his way without incident through a thorny political issue that the more serious papers had felt certain would take him at least twice as long, and would likely end in failure. In every other area of his life he not only considered himself well prepared, but fully capable of steering events to the conclusions he preferred.

And in this case, he once again had the strangest sensation. Strange, but familiar over the course of these last couple of months. Despite the familiarity, it took him long moments to realize it was him feeling like some kind of fool.

Again.

He had never felt like this before this woman had entered his life, and he had no wish to feel it again. But it did not go away as she stared back at him. And when he said nothing, she continued.

"She said that in some ways, your father was lovely," Helene told him. And everything inside of him was on high alert, warning him that he wasn't going to like whatever she was about to say. Or perhaps it was that something in him knew it would be one more of these explosions she was far too good at doling out. He wanted to tell her to stop, but he worried that would seem like a weakness. And worse, that she wouldn't. Especially as her expression shifted into *compassion*. "But only if he wasn't crossed. Get on his bad side, however, and he could be vindictive. Petty. She said he had a nasty temper."

He did not want to hear this. He could not hear this. There was no point digging up a dead man—much less that temper of his that Gianluca had long believed had been saved for his family alone.

Because it was unthinkable that anyone else might know of those black rages.

If they did—if anyone did—then everything his family was, everything *he was*, could be no more than another lie.

He ran a hand through his hair and hated that

he was betraying his own agitation. "And you believe that I am the person to whom you should repeat this bit of fantasy? From a woman discarded by a king?"

There was too much of that compassion, all over her. "Why would she lie?"

It would have been different if Helene had seemed insistent. If she had poked or prodded in some way. If she had treated this like some kind of a grand exposé. Instead, she sounded...

Not sad. Not quite. Rather as if she felt sorry for him, and Gianluca would obviously have taken immediate exception to such an outrage, but having never experienced it before, he found that the best he could do was stand there, wondering why it felt so much like a heart attack.

"If she wished to profit off such claims, she would have done so many years ago, in the wake of her actual relationship with your father," Helene pointed out when he did not reply, sounding quite reasonable. "She would have made a tremendous amount of money. She said she had people at her door night and day, bothering her parents and chasing her friends. While she was dating your father and then twice as many after. She could easily have dined out on her stories of dating the King for years. Instead she said nothing. And her reward was finding herself cast as a participant in a love triangle she had never taken part in."

"Why are we standing here in the cold, litigating ancient history?" Gianluca demanded. "I lived through the aftermath of this, Helene. I do not need a primer."

"You never speak much about your father, did you know that?" When he glared at her, she smiled, though her gaze remained direct and solemn. "Lady Lorenza didn't wish to speak about him either. Do you know what she told me?"

"I do not."

One of the reasons this woman was so confounding was that she ignored him completely when she chose. As she did now. "She told me, with a sincerity that made her voice shake, that her relationship with your father had been a whirlwind. So wildly intense that she'd never quite known where she stood. She'd never known if she truly loved him or if she was swept up in his insistence that *he* loved *her*. And he was the King!"

"You might be surprised how little some women find themselves in awe of kings," Gianluca said darkly. "It is the scourge of modernity."

She acknowledged that with the faintest smile, but kept going. "But she found that breaking up with him felt like a relief, not a disaster, no matter the carrying-on in the gossip columns. And then she finally met her husband, who she'd been promised to when she was young but had not met as an adult. She said that the moment she did, that she had ever imagined that a royal three-ring circus—her words—could have anything to do with her was a joke. Because it seems that she and her husband have been quietly and completely in love with each other since first sight."

"Did you read this in one of your fairy stories?"

"Where I didn't read it was in the tabloids, where she was cast as a villain at best. And it certainly didn't stop your father from trying to involve her in his games."

Gianluca was rapidly reaching his limit. "My father did not play games, Helene. If you wish to muck about in other people's history, I suggest you get your facts straight."

"He didn't need to play games when he had the tabloids to do it for him," Helene said softly. "And look. He's been dead for ten years and now you do it too."

And that, Gianluca decided, was his breaking point.

That was *enough*—

But he was the King of Fiammetta, so he certainly could not break in public. He could not let the things that roared inside of him out.

He did the next best thing, bowing curtly to his queen and then ushering her back inside, so they could finish out the rest of this formal evening without becoming the only story that would be told about the event.

Later they sat in the car on the way back to the palace the way they always did, and he knew that he was not alone in thinking of the many times by now that he had closed the distance between them. Or she had. The many times they had found their way beneath each other's formal clothes to find the truth about themselves beneath.

Or *a* truth, he amended.

And that was not the way this night was going to go.

Not when he couldn't get the things she'd said about his father out of his head.

When they got to their apartments, she turned toward her own rooms and he did not stop her. But he didn't go to his bedchamber either. He dismissed his staff, finding his way to one of his private studies where he was drawn, unerringly, to a framed old picture he kept on the wall.

It was a famous photograph, one that had been published all over the world. It showed the young, vibrant King Alvize playing with his young son one summer afternoon in the palace gardens. Queen Elettra sat behind them, laughing happily in the sunlight.

A vision of a happy family, everyone had agreed. Everyone so beautiful, so covered in joy, so perfect in every way.

But it was all a lie.

One he had been telling himself ever since.

Though he had to have been only five years old, Gianluca could still remember that afternoon clearly, though he rarely allowed himself to stick his fingers in that particular wound. He didn't remember this moment, captured forever on film. But here, tonight, he let himself remember his mother flirting with the photographer—or rather, that his father had accused her of flirting later. From those actual, long-ago moments in the sun, what he remembered most was the terrifying force of his father's attention. And the agony he had felt to perform perfectly for the man, lest it be his fault that Alvize's good mood go away.

As it so often was.

It was not a good memory, that photograph.

Yet he had chosen to keep it where he could see it, always, though he hadn't allowed himself to really think about that day in years.

And it was only now, standing here after one more confounding evening with his own queen, that Gianluca questioned himself. He was forced to wonder if the reason he held on to this photograph, and kept it displayed where he would see it often, wasn't for any sense of nostalgia as he imagined others might think.

As he had convinced himself he felt.

Because he kept hoping that if he looked at this picture long enough, he would forget what had actually happened between the people in that photo and instead see what everyone else did.

Or what he had hoped they did.

A happy family. A sweet moment. A light so bright that winter could never come again. No rain, no snow, not even the faintest shadow.

He made a low noise that he didn't recognize as himself. Then he wheeled around, making his way almost blindly to the door that connected his apartments to Helene's. The hallway was too long. There were too many rooms.

He didn't *recognize* himself and that was impossible.

Because he knew who he was. The whole world had known who he was before he'd drawn his first breath. He had been born to his role and there was nothing else.

Surely there could be nothing else.

He found her sitting at the vanity in her dressing room, taking down her hair. She had dismissed her staff too, as she usually did, so used was she to fending for herself.

Tonight he was glad of it. He walked up behind her, watching the shifting emotions as they played through the gold in her gaze, the softness of her wide mouth.

The graveness of her expression.

"Gianluca," she began.

"You have said quite enough tonight, *mia regina*," he said, and it, too, was someone else's voice, rough and raw.

Helene swiveled around on her seat as he drew close, and that suited him. He went down before her and ran his hand up her legs and over her thighs, urging them apart as he moved to kneel between them.

She whispered his name again, but he could feel the heat of her.

When he leaned in, he could smell her, too. The hint of the perfume she used and beneath it, far more potent, that scent that was only hers. That scent that made his mouth water and his sex ache.

He shifted her, tilting her hips up so he could drape her knees over his shoulders and spread her wide for him.

Like dessert.

She did not bother with undergarments any

longer, because they only ever got in the way, and Gianluca was glad of it.

As he did not want to think. He did not want to interrogate the strange things he felt, or wonder why it was that he had locked them away inside himself all this time. Too many unwieldy truths. Too many intensities he did not wish to face.

He did not understand how she had managed to find the key to all these things.

But he didn't want to *think*, he wanted to *feel*.

Instead, he could hold her rounded bottom in his hands. He could get his mouth into all that silky heat, that sweet delirium, that he thought about more often than he should. In places where his thoughts should have been far away from such private matters.

But he was here now. He licked his way into her and that roar of longing and relief soared in him. He lifted her off the vanity so he could lay her out on the floor. So he could really dedicate himself to what he was doing and so when she thrashed beneath him, as she began to do quickly, she would not knock over anything or hurt herself in any way.

Gianluca did not choose to question himself.

He did not ask why it was he settled down, took his time, and ignored the demands of his own body as he made her sob and moan beneath him. As he took her to that edge, and teased her there, again and again.

Too many times to count.

When he could take no more, and she had tears tracking down the sides of her face from the force of the many times she'd come apart, he finally freed only the hungriest part of himself. He pressed himself to her, working his way inside her.

She was still a tight fit. She was always a tight fit, no matter how many times he made her buck and sob, and something caught at him—

But he couldn't hold on to it, because she was so soft, so scalding hot, and it was all he could do to thrust into her, over and over, until there was a hitch in her breathing again.

Until she was lifting her hips to his and arching up against him all over again.

Until she shattered once more, and took him with her.

And it took them both some time to find themselves again, lying in an inelegant heap on the floor of her dressing room.

"Do you have more to share with me?" Gianluca asked her, lifting a brow at her disheveled state, her hair a mess and every part of her flushed. "Tabloid stories, perhaps?"

And when all Helene could do was laugh,

he carried her to the bedroom and started all over again.

Gianluca congratulated himself in the following days for finally understanding that there was only way to handle his wife. The more orgasms he gave her, the less she seemed to feel the urge to say such provocative things to him.

And if there was a part of him that missed the way she challenged him, he dismissed it.

Because this was better, surely.

This was what he'd wanted all along.

He might have actually found his footing in this marriage.

He assured himself that, finally, he had.

But one night, after they hosted a party in one of the palace's private rooms, Gianluca stayed afterward to talk with some of the guests a bit more privately so that they could hammer out a delicate arrangement that would leave the crown out of a particular business issue.

He expected it to take some while, but was thrilled when he was able to wrap it up and tie it in a bow quickly.

Because while Gianluca had only and ever been a creature of duty, forever in service to the crown, he was learning to resent it when those duties took him away from his wife.

And from wielding those tools he had finally learned how to use properly.

Yet when he let himself into the Queen's apartments, Helene wasn't there. He headed back to his own rooms, assuming he might find her in his bed instead. But she was not there either.

He walked out to the guards who waited at the entrance to the King and Queen's apartments, for none could pass without their knowledge.

"I'm looking for the Queen," he said.

And then, to his astonishment, he watched members of his own guard exchange a look, and then...not answer their king immediately.

One stared at the ground. The other stared straight ahead.

Gianluca felt a kind of storm in him, first a hint of far-off thunder. "I beg your pardon. Was I unclear? Where is the Queen?"

The guard with his head up cleared his throat. "My most abject apologies, Your Majesty. But the Queen expressly commanded us to keep silent about her whereabouts."

Gianluca merely raised a brow. He did not point out that his wishes superseded all others, always.

He did not have to. If he *did* have to, then perhaps it was time he abdicated.

But sure enough, all he needed to do was stare. The man let out a long sigh, the other one groaned, and they confessed.

And that was how Gianluca found himself stalking through the palace, then out into the rear gardens. He crossed the sprawling palace complex with what felt like murderous steps, hardly noticing the cold night, until he found himself at the door to the dower cottage once more.

He did not permit the guard to announce him.

Instead, he moved in a seething silence into the house, following the sound of voices he knew only too well.

And there he found them, sitting close together on the settee. With all those pictures on the mantel arrayed above them, another set of carefully curated lies.

His mother was dressed, suggesting this visit was no surprise though it was after midnight. And his own treacherous queen had not bothered to change from dinner, so it was tempting to imagine this was formal, the two of them talking the way that they were…

Except they were clasping each other's hands as if they were friends, and Gianluca felt something in him tear open at the sight.

He told himself it was betrayal.

"What," he bit out, and perhaps he enjoyed the way they both jolted a little too much at the sound of his voice, "in the name of all that is holy is going on here?"

His mother looked instantly defiant, but that was typical Elettra. He would deal with her later. He kept his gaze on Helene, expecting to see a look of guilt on her lovely, lying face.

But he did not.

Instead, if she was still startled by his sudden appearance, she didn't show it. All she did was shift so she could train that gold-tipped gaze of hers on him.

"What does it look like?" she asked, with that unimpeachable serenity of hers that might very well be what put him in his grave, no abdication required. "I decided it was high time I met my mother-in-law."

CHAPTER TEN

HELENE COULD FEEL the older woman's hands trembling in hers, so she didn't let go. Instead, she held on tight—but she didn't take her eyes off her husband.

Who she thought was the most stubborn man she'd ever met, and she'd grown up under the foot of a man who had redefined the term *single-minded*.

"And before you tell me that I have nothing to talk about with my own mother-in-law," she continued, because she by now could read the kinds of storms that moved through his gaze, "I'll thank you to allow me to decide such things on my own. It isn't up to you."

"When will you understand?" Gianluca's voice was almost soft, and she knew that meant he was at his most dangerous. "It is all up to me. This is my kingdom, Helene. I was born to rule it. My word is law. Which is likely to prove that to you?"

"Be cruel to me if you must, Gianluca," his mother said then. She shifted so that she could put an arm around her daughter-in-law's shoulders. "Don't turn yourself into a bully. Hasn't he already taken enough?"

Helene was absurdly touched by that. She had first come to see Elettra not long after she'd initially realized she was pregnant.

My dear, Elettra had said when Helene had snuck over to see her, *you must not know my son very well if you think that there is any way to ingratiate yourself to him through me.*

I'm trying to ingratiate myself to you, Your Majesty, Helene had replied, with a perfect curtsy. *And much as I'd like to be friends, I have a deeper purpose.*

She had not announced that she intended to get to the truth of things. Still, Elettra nodded as if she knew. And they had enjoyed an afternoon tea, which happened to be Helene's most favorite meal of all.

The boarding school I went to took tea very seriously, she'd told Gianluca's mother. *We were in Switzerland, and the headmistress was quite ferociously German, but she told us all that a great deal of the world was arranged around a proper British tea service. The feminine part of the world, I mean. And it was a language she insisted we learn, if only because calling for a tea service during the middle of an unpleasant discussion gives everyone something to do. And therefore can shift the discussion to something more pleasant automatically.*

There is a reason, Elettra had said with a murmur, *that the British were so good at holding on to their empire for a time.*

Helene did not think that colonialism was predicated on tea, but she also did not intend to argue with the Dowager Queen of Fiammetta.

So instead, she and this wary, watchful, beautiful woman whose son looked almost exactly like her, sipped at their Darjeeling. They nibbled at cunning petit fours and did not have to choose between scones and crumpets—the way Elettra suggested Gianluca had always done—for both were on offer.

And as she'd risen to leave, Elettra had studied her teacup as if it held all the wisdom of the world.

Do you make my son happy? she'd asked. And then she'd looked up, with a smile. *It is not that I think he is particularly capable of happiness. It is more that I'm wondering if you've managed to convince him that he could be. That it is even remotely possible.*

Helene had shrugged helplessly. *I don't know,* she had said honestly.

They had met twice more after that, and while

each visit was pleasant, they started doing a bit of digging, Elettra and Helene. Some comparing of notes. And Helene had intended to raise the subject of his mother with Gianluca.

Eventually.

She couldn't say she was sorry that he had appeared here tonight. No matter how thunderous he looked.

And that was putting it mildly.

"You will not speak of my father, Madam," Gianluca bit out, that black glare of his on Elettra.

Helene did not think it through. She stood, as if prepared to put her body between Gianluca and Elettra if necessary. And she knew the instant she did it that he would not take to it kindly.

He did not. His eyes widened in affront.

"This is your mother, Gianluca," she reminded her husband. "How is it you have managed to forget that?"

As he took a step toward her, Helene felt her heart catch in her chest. Because the lie she believed least was that he was as cold and as remote as he sometimes behaved.

She knew different. She'd *felt* different.

This was the man who'd become her lover.

This was the man who was still obsessed with the absurd notion that she had lied about her innocence—but who she sometimes caught looking at her with a very nearly soft expression on his face when he thought she was asleep.

Maybe she was putting too much stock in those moments. Maybe she wanted them to mean something they didn't, a necklace of connected baubles, little threads for a tapestry only she would ever see.

Helene had to believe otherwise.

She had to, for her own heart—and for her child.

"I never forget my mother," Gianluca told her darkly. "I never forget her betrayals. The mockery she made of her position, of the crown, and of everything else I hold dear. I do not need you to wade into matters that do not concern you and make them more complicated."

But Helene did not back down, because she could see beneath that darkness. She could see the hurt in him. She could feel it like an ache in her own bones. She thought of a little boy who believed what he was told, because he had no reason not to, and she hurt, too. "I can think of very little that concerns me more."

"I will deal with you later," Gianluca told Helene, though his gaze shifted to Elettra. "My mother and I need to refresh our memories."

Elettra stood, then, and somehow Helene knew that she was the only one here who saw the way the other woman trembled. And also how she hid it.

She met and held her son's gaze. "My memory is perfectly clear," she told him.

And every single thing Helene had ever learned urged her to sit down. To do as she was told. To retreat in the moment, so she might live to fight another day. To bend, choose silence, and utilize softness as a weapon.

Helene had always been so good at these things.

But she was carrying a baby. She was going to be a mother.

She could not live with herself if she did not fight for the life she wanted. The life her child deserved.

Because what good was the magic she and Gianluca made between them if everything else was poisoned? And though she had intended to simply prove, over time, that she could not be the liar he believed her to be—through her character, through her works, through the way she loved him—she felt as if she was running out of that time now. For there was no way she could bring a child into the world when her own husband truly believed that, at heart, she was a liar.

She knew it started here, in this quiet little cottage, where another woman branded a liar and a cheat had waited all this time. Not always out of sight. Not always quietly. Not always according to the principles Helene felt certain Elettra knew as well as she did, when it came to handling powerful men and highly weighted marriages.

"Do you know what I asked your mother?" Helene began.

Gianluca let out that bitter laugh of his. "I shudder to think."

"She asked me a question no one has thought to ask me in a very long while," Elettra said, and she looked almost wistful. "And for once I felt I could truly answer."

"I don't understand the purpose of this," Gianluca thundered then, as if the storm in him had spilled over. "Is it not enough that I allow you both to live here, insulated from the lies you have told and the damage you've done? What more is it that you want?"

It was not clear which woman he was speaking to, Helene saw.

Which was the problem.

"I asked your mother if she really had cheated on your father," Helene said quietly, well aware that the words made Gianluca jerk as if she'd kicked him in the gut.

And it was hard not to go to him, but she couldn't. She wouldn't. This was her chance to carve out a better life for all of them here…if only he would let himself see it.

"Not why. Not how. Not, *what could you be thinking?* and so on." Elettra laughed, and the sound coming from her was not bitter at all. "I was stunned. In thirty years, no one has ever doubted that I am guilty as charged, in every possible way."

"Because you are." Gianluca's voice was so low. His eyes were so dark.

Helene still stood between the two of them, and she lifted a hand as if extending it toward Gianluca.

She did not expect him to take it. But it still cut that he didn't.

"But what if there was a deeper lie?" she asked him, and shook her head at the look of something like bewilderment on her face. "I couldn't get the things Lady Lorenza told me out of my mind. The things she did not want to say about your father's character, and how that, juxtaposed with a happy life she leads outside of the spotlight, made me wonder. And I started to think about what it is that lies do. How they can transform everything."

"Do you need a lesson in this?" Gianluca demanded, but he did not sound like himself. He sounded…torn.

She had to hope it was enough.

"I am a walking object lesson in this, Gianluca," Helene replied. "But first, imagine this. A young girl marries an overwhelmingly powerful man. He is older than her, the king of everything, and he quickly makes it clear that he will only tolerate the strictest possible control on her at all times. As if she is little more than a trophy. All his, to do with as he wishes."

Gianluca ran his hands over his face. "Is this one of your fairy tales, Helene?" He dropped his hands and eyed his mother. "Do you think this version of events will work?"

"The thing about tabloids," Helene said softly, before Elettra could snap back at her son, "is that they don't have anything interesting to say about people who find happiness and quiet lives on the other side of the glare. So why would they continually drag Lorenza into all those stories about King Alvize and his marriage? Unless, of course, someone far more powerful than an ex-girlfriend who made no attempt at any point to capitalize on her relationship to the crown, was feeding it to them?"

Gianluca's dark gaze moved to Elettra, then back to Helene, as hard as a fist. "What are you saying?"

She thought he might know, but she kept going anyway. "Imagine Lorenza was less the great love of your father's life, and more the only person who had ever dared defy him. Would he want revenge? That was the second question I asked your mother."

Helene glanced at Elettra, who swallowed. Hard. But she did not back down.

"One night," the older woman said, "your father was in one of his moods. You remember how he was." And Helene thought that Gianluca's silence then said more than any protestation could have. "One of the aides told me it was because Lorenza had announced her pregnancy. Alvize did not like this. He was ranting and raving, and I was all of twenty. Heavily pregnant myself, with his heir, and I thought I'd heard quite enough of the Lady Lorenza to last me a lifetime." A shadow crossed her face, as if she was looking in a very old mirror. "I suggested that he was jealous. I pointed out that she couldn't make it any plainer that she'd moved on."

Gianluca let out a sigh that told Helene that all the inferences she'd made about his father, about his family, were true.

Elettra looked down for a moment. "That was unwise. But I didn't learn my lesson. He made me sorry enough that night, but I got to thinking in the way that angry young girls do. He'd hurt my feelings and I thought I could hurt his, too." She lifted her head, and Helene saw her son in the way she held herself. "Maybe what I needed was a little leverage. Maybe I needed him to think that I was something he could lose too. Maybe then he would treat me with a little more respect."

Gianluca muttered something beneath his breath. Helene held hers.

"Your grandmother was still alive, and while she and I never had a bond as some do, she had told me very early in my marriage that she had never known a man who did not benefit from imagining there was some competition." She smiled when Gianluca made another dark, low noise. "So one time, when he was raging on about Lorenza and how it was obvious to anyone who looked that she was living her life *at* him, I asked if he would show the same interest in me if I ever decided to break up with him. Or, in the way of so many royals, not break up with him at all, but move on all the same."

Gianluca looked shaken. "You did not say this."

Elettra held her son's gaze. "I did."

"That was a remarkably foolish thing to do." And Gianluca sounded as close to stricken as Helene had ever heard him.

"Did you ever wonder why a man with your father's temper, raging down the palace, somehow sat idly by while his wife betrayed him so publicly and repeatedly?" When Elettra laughed this time, it was a brittle sound. "When I woke up, it was to discover that he had knocked me out cold in two ways. The first with a backhand. And the second with the papers. The stories of my first affair were all over the papers."

Gianluca flinched as if he'd taken a blow himself. He was breathing too heavily, ghosts in his eyes, and a dawning, horrible new knowledge. "While you were pregnant. With me."

Elettra nodded slowly. Deliberately. "And then, my darling son, he had a weapon. One he could use as he pleased. When I spoke out, or dared defend myself. When I misbehaved or when you did—every time, he invented a new lover. I lost count. And for good measure, he made certain to suggest that, perhaps, Lorenza's son was his too. That Lorenza was part of the triangle that existed only in his head. I'm sure he hoped that, at the very least, he could wreck her marriage as well."

Helene moved toward Gianluca then, putting a hand on his arm that he did not seem to feel, too lost was he in the past.

"You are not to blame for believing this," she told him fiercely. "You had no reason not to. He was your father. He was the King. From everything I've heard, he was terrifying."

"And charming," Elettra said, her voice thick.

"He could be so charming, out in public. That was what made you imagine he wasn't a monster. But then we would come home and he would be hideous to me and unkind to you too, and I didn't know what else to do. I knew he would never let you leave. So I stayed. And then he died and I still stayed, even though you did not want me near, because I could not bear to leave you. I still can't."

Helene watched something wash over Gianluca then, like a body blow. And there was the distinct sheen of vulnerability in his gaze when he looked at her. Anguish. Despair.

But then, just as quickly, it was shuttered again.

He took a step back. He shook his head once, then again. "No," he said, very distinctly. "These are lies upon lies upon lies. I will not let you drown me in the swamp of yours, Madam."

Though Helene was not certain whether he spoke to her, or his mother.

And then it didn't matter. "You have outstayed your welcome," he threw at his mother.

She only sighed as she sat again, looking smaller than before. "Like father, like son," she murmured.

It was a blow, and it landed. For a moment Gianluca looked as if it might take him down—

But he shook it off.

Then he was taking Helene by the arm, and she let him because she knew what he apparently did not—which was that there was no going back from this moment. There was no pretending that the whole of his life, and all of his beliefs about his family, weren't stacked precariously on the lies and petty jealousies of a very small man on his big throne.

She waited until they were out in the middle palace complex, with gardens on all sides, the late winter night above them, and no guards nearby to hear.

"It's surprising that you claim to be so allergic to lies," she began.

"Yet you keep on spinning them," he ground out.

Helene stopped walking, and Gianluca whirled so he could face her. And she thought he looked nothing like himself tonight. He looked as close to disheveled as she'd ever seen him. His eyes were wild. His face was twisted.

This should have scared her. But it didn't.

Gianluca didn't scare her at all.

That wasn't to say he couldn't break her heart. That he hadn't already. That he wouldn't again. But she didn't *fear* him.

His own mother had not been able to say the same about the King she'd been married to.

"Why are you so sure that I lied to you on

our wedding night?" Helene demanded of him now, out here in the dark and the cold. With no trace of her usual calm, her hard-won ease and grace. There was no room for that now. "What is your evidence? Or is it just you have always been taught that women are liars?"

"It has nothing to do with what I have or haven't been taught," he threw at her. "It is as simple as this, Helene. Every time I touch you, every time I go near you at all, you burst into flame. What virgin does this?"

"This virgin," she shot back at him. And she did not shrink. She did not dip her head or avert her eyes. Tonight she was done with strategy, with waiting for the right moment. What moments were left? This was her life. This was her child's whole world they were discussing, whether he knew it or not. "This woman, who has been in love with you since the very first moment she set eyes on you, and not because you're a king. You could have been the gardener, for all I cared. I looked up, you were there, and everything changed. I burst into flames every time you touch me because of the fire between us. It's *ours*, Gianluca."

He looked wild, but she couldn't stop.

"I have never touched another man," she told him, as if they were standing at another altar. But this one was far more critical. "I have no interest in other men. And no, I can't prove that. Just as your poor mother couldn't prove to anyone that she was the innocent victim of your father's schemes. The same way poor Lady Lorenza couldn't either. Deep down, Gianluca, I think you know this already."

He made a sound that was more animal than man. He speared his fingers into his hair and wrenched himself away, turning from her—but he only walked one step, then two.

She thought that when he spoke again he would sound as unsteady as she felt, but he didn't.

Helene would never know how he didn't when she wasn't sure her own heart would ever be the same.

"Do you think I will wait to send you away?" he asked in that voice of his that was all soft fury. "You are a disruptive presence. I will not allow it. I will pack you off to my grandmother's mountain retreat at dawn."

"No," Helene said.

She didn't plan it. The word simply slipped out, shocking her with its power.

Perhaps it shouldn't have shocked her. After all, it was the only word the Institut had always forbid them to use. They were taught to go under, over, or through.

The point of being obliging, the teachers

would always tell them, *is to appear so even when you're being nothing of the kind.*

It is your appearance of meekness that is your greatest weapon, the headmistress had told them, time and again.

But out here in the dark, with clouds scudding across the waxing moon, Helene stopped being meek.

She stopped worrying about weapons.

Because she already had one and he didn't even know it.

It was high time he did.

"No?" Gianluca repeated, as if he'd never heard the word before. "I don't recall asking for your permission."

"I'm pregnant, Gianluca," she told him, and she did nothing to soften the blow of those words. She did nothing to cushion him or protect him. This was not the time for softness. "And that means a great many things, but most of all this. You have to decide what kind of life your child is going to have. You have to decide what kind of family you are going to give him or her."

She thought he said her name, but she wasn't finished.

Helene drifted closer to him, tipped her head back, and looked him in the eye. "Starting right now."

CHAPTER ELEVEN

SHE COULD NOT have said anything that could have cut him in half more neatly.

Gianluca stared down at her, feeling as if he'd fallen from some great height and landed hard on his back, knocking the wind straight out of him.

This time, it was far more than the usual unsteadiness in Helene's presence.

This time it felt like a mortal wound.

He could hear her breathing, or maybe it was him, his own wind kind of stalling deep inside him. He felt a kind of sundering, deep within.

He could think of no other word for it.

He wanted to reach out and pull Helene close. He wanted to sink down onto his knees before her, put his hands on that belly he knew so well, yet had not sensed any changes in.

He wanted to make it clear to her, however he could, that he had no intention of being the kind of father his own had been—

But he did not do any one of those things.

Because wasn't he on track to being *exactly* like his father?

And tonight, as the clouds danced across the moon, he couldn't pretend his father was the innocent victim any longer. He couldn't pretend he hadn't spent most of his adult life tamping down on the memories that he'd long ago decided could not possibly help him.

His father had been cold and distant, violent on bad days, and then he had been dead.

When there were others around, he had been handsome and awe-inspiring. He had seemed everything a king and a father should have been—but it had never lasted.

Hoping it might had been almost as bad as weathering one of Alvize's rages.

Gianluca had learned how to hide. He had escaped to school. He had stopped *hoping*. When he finished school, he dedicated himself to a life of preparation for the crown. He made himself a beacon of duty.

He made himself the man he'd wished his father really had been.

Anything to be someone other than that terrified small boy.

Anything to be something besides a victim.

Because if he was a victim, then it was far more possible that his mother was, too.

His mother, who had stuck around. Who had

never hidden away, nor run. Elettra had instead remained seemingly unapologetic. She had never corrected the record. She had never explained.

Gianluca had thought it was defiance—he had wanted to believe it was—but out here in the cold tonight, it seemed a lot more like dignity.

And after tonight, he was going to have to face the fact that while he knew his father all too well, he knew his own mother not at all.

It all seemed to jumble around inside of him. Mothers and fathers. Children. Helene, who was simply waiting in that way of hers. Not quite so maddeningly serene tonight, but watching him closely—as if she already knew exactly what would happen inside him in the face of her announcement.

He suspected she might.

She was his queen. His wife.

She was going to be the mother of his child.

The child that he had declared he would treat precisely as he had been treated. When he'd said that, he'd been focused on his work. How he'd turned out. What had become of him, not how it had felt.

But tonight he could remember that scared little boy who had wanted only his mother.

And whatever it was that had come asunder inside of him before broke apart even further now.

Gianluca took a step back, then another. He

was aware that he was staggering like a drunk man, but he could not seem to stop himself.

"Helene," he managed to grit out. "Helene, *mia regina*, I do not think you understand…"

But when he stepped back again, she came forward. She came straight to him as if she was sure that he would welcome her easily.

As if he had not been keeping her at arm's distance from the start.

He thought of what she'd said to him here, that she'd had the courage to say it when he had not. That they had looked at each other in a garden in Provence, the smell of lavender in the air and bees buzzing lazily as they would, and everything had changed.

They had changed, and theirs were not the sort of lives that allowed for such things.

There had been no place to put something so overwhelming. So mad and wild and intense.

"I had to keep you in your proper place." He would never know how he forced those words free from the constriction in his chest, his throat. And he could hear how it sounded, there in the cool night air in the shadow of the palace. "I don't mean that in the way you think I do."

"Then tell me what you mean," she said quietly.

Gianluca blew out a breath, as if that would help. Or loosen his chest enough to speak, anyway. "My father, who I wanted very badly to think of as a good man, called me into the throne room and told me how the world works. I was ten. Looking back, I do not think this was because he was seized with the urge to parent his only child. I believe it was because he thought he could leverage me against my mother."

And it wasn't lost on him that the word *mother* sounded thick and little used on his tongue.

Because it was.

Helene moved closer, keeping that gaze of hers so steady on his. As if all he really needed to do was follow the gold there, brighter than the moon. "He explained to me that the King especially must keep everything partitioned. And I'm not sure I thought much of him as a man, though I wished I could, but I thought he was a decent king. And after his death, when my mother seemed to get more and more erratic by the day—"

He stopped himself. Because everything inside him was spinning around and around, and he could not be certain he knew anything. Not even what he would have said, only a few hours ago, was the inevitability of Elettra's lust for the spotlight.

Because it was possible—it was more than just *possible*—that it had never been that at all.

"I think you can grieve people in a variety

of ways," Helene said quietly. "And not all of them are palatable to others. I don't know why we think they should be."

Gianluca tried his best to focus. Not on his mother's grief, but on the things he needed to say to this woman. His wife and queen.

This woman who would make him a father.

"I was sure that I could handle you," he told her then, his voice low and rough, not cultured at all. "I told myself that the connection between us was simply…icing on the cake. Instead of what it really was."

She nodded, solemnly, and did not pretend that she didn't know exactly what he meant.

"And then, on our wedding night, it was all too much." He raked his hands through his hair again. "I thought I could control that, too. I needed to control everything, Helene, and when I couldn't, I seized on the only possible explanation I could find for why everything between us was…"

He couldn't find the right word.

But she could. She gazed at him, all solemn gold and a kind of certainty that made his heart thud against his ribs. "Magic."

Gianluca had no defense against her. Why had he ever imagined otherwise?

"And so instead of telling you that I was terribly afraid that I'd fallen in love, when the only thing I had ever seen was its death throes, I chose instead to accuse you. I worked for years to block my father's offense from my memory, because the truth is that he never loved anything. Not Lady Lorenza. Not my mother. And certainly not me."

"But your mother did," Helene whispered, as if she already knew this confession was so terrible, he had never admitted it even to himself. "She loved you no matter how horrible you were to her."

Something old and painful cracked inside of him. "She did."

"That's what mothers do," Helene told him, standing there before him as if she was impervious to the mountain air. "That's what my mother did. There were no public recriminations, not like here. But you've met my father. He was always a cold man. Before my mother died, commenting on his moods was like the weather, nothing more. After she died, I had to cater to those moods, and that was different. Because a parent who doesn't love you, or loves himself far more, allows for no imperfections. Every step put wrong is a mark against you and a stain upon their name. I learned to be spotless."

"It is as if you and I were raised by the same man," Gianluca said roughly, though the words still hurt. His throat was still too tight. Every bone in his body ached. And his ribs could not seem to contain his heart. "Though I find myself envious that you had the time you did with your mother. My father saw to it that I could not have even that. I was sent away to school so soon that I heard stories about my mother from my classmates, and so she was framed in my mind as the harlot he painted her to be, even then."

"I don't think I really understood until this moment," Helene whispered, "that my sweet mother spoke to me of fairy tales and Prince Charmings, not because she wanted to inure me to my fate, but because on some level she must have believed that she would be able to sway my father from his path." She pulled in a breath gone ragged. "Because it never occurred to me until now that fathers who truly love their daughters do not sell them for clout. Not even to kings."

And then with the weight of all of this clear and obvious between them, Gianluca sank at last to his knees.

When he reached for Helene, he found that she was crying. Tears rolled down her cheeks, and splashed on his fingers. This from a woman who he had never seen cry, not outside the bedroom.

"I did this to you," he said gruffly. "I have stolen your reserve."

"That is nothing but a mask I wear," she whispered, dashing her fingers across her eyes, though more tears followed all the same.

"I don't think I knew until just recently that I could take it off."

And Gianluca thought of the day he had proposed to her. How he had come once again to that château in Provence, sweeping into the old house in all his state, with all his aides and staff. They had conducted the last of his talks with her father—all about money, naturally, not a word about his daughter's well-being or happiness—and then the many contracts had been signed, one after the next.

It had been a business meeting like any other.

Then they had all sat down to an excruciatingly formal lunch, where Helene ate nothing, her father made off-color jokes, and, at last, Gianluca had stood, inclined his head, and announced that it would please him greatly if she would consent to become the Queen of Fiammetta.

Tonight, he took her hands in his. He pulled her close so he could kiss each one, and then he circled her hips so he could lean in and place a kiss to her belly.

It felt like starting over.

So that was what he did.

"I believe you," he told her.

Gianluca did not think about kings, not his father nor himself. He thought about Helene. And whatever man he was, hidden beneath all that perfection he had imagined he could attain when what he wanted most was this.

To breathe a little while and hold her while he did it.

No wonder she had scared him so much he'd turned tyrant instead of facing that he, all along, was the problem between them. He was the lie.

"I think I always knew you did not lie to me, no matter what I tried to tell myself. For how could you be so perfect in every way, even in bed? I could not make sense of it. I've had my staff scouring all of Europe to uncover your deceit, yet they continue to come up empty. And I think that you are very wise, Helene. Far smarter than you sometimes let on. But I do not think that even you can escape the kind of scrutiny that I have given your past."

"That is all very logical," she said dryly. "I'm so pleased you had your reasons."

And as he knelt there on the cold ground, he felt a huge thing move in him. For a brief moment he thought that perhaps he was dying, after all—

But it was a laugh.

A deep, surging laugh from the deepest part of him.

He let it come. He threw back his head and let it out, and it felt good. Right.

Just like her.

"Is that a hint of temper I hear in your voice?"

he asked Helene. "Are you, a graduate of the Institut and the Queen of Fiammetta...actually displaying your true thoughts to me?"

She wiped at her face again, seeming as shaken by the sound of his laugh as he was. "It appears to be that kind of night."

Gianluca knew it was. So he pulled her down with him until they were both kneeling on the earth, as if he was trying to re-create the day they'd met. But better this time. More honest.

Maybe he was.

"This is our beginning, you and me," he told her intently. "For I have been a fool of epic proportions. Starting with the fact that I have never properly asked you to be my wife and tumbling on from there, so let me be perfectly clear, Helene. I have never been the same since the moment I saw you. I would never have said I believed in love at first sight, but I know that it can be nothing else. I would have told you that I have no idea what love might be, but you have showed me, haven't you?"

This was not a real question. She had. Every day, she had. She had not threatened him like his father. She had not challenged him to think the worst of her like his mother. She had simply loved him, and in so doing, unraveled him from the inside out.

He hadn't even realized she was doing it.

Gianluca smoothed his hand over her cheek, then let his fingers find their way into those wild, dark curls he adored. "You have weathered my disgraceful behavior. You had every reason to throw temper tantrums, break things, perhaps even leave me here in this kingdom of mine, but you did not. You stayed by my side. You listened to me speak ill of you with compassion. You have showed me, again and again, that love is far more complicated than I could have imagined. And far more beautiful. And so all I can hope is that I have the opportunity to prove to you that I can love you back, in the way that you deserve, and somehow make up for these things I've done to you."

"Just because you didn't see my reactions doesn't mean I didn't have them," Helene whispered, her tears still falling. "There was a part of me that wanted to leave. There was a part of me that wished, desperately, that I could hate you. There is always this thing in me that is a product of how I was raised and what I was taught, that urges me to make myself disappear in plain sight. To be obliging, reserved, and to live behind this mask of good manners even if it suffocates me."

"Promise me," he said, dark and intent, "*promise me* that you will leave that mask at our bedroom door. That, alone, you and I will not be a king and a queen, but a man and a woman."

"A husband," she whispered. "And a wife."

"I am so sorry, *mia regina*," he told her, from every part of him. "*Cuore mio*, my heart, I promise you that I will do everything within my power to make myself worthy of your forgiveness."

"Just love me," she whispered back. "And I will love you back. We will forgive each other whether we deserve it or not, and we will teach our child not only how to love, but how to be loved as we were not." And she leaned closer, her expression grave again, no matter that her eyes were still so wet. "But Gianluca, I will not be going away to any prison on a mountainside. And I will not send my baby away at the age of six. I don't imagine I will like it very much at sixteen."

"Helene, my wife, *mia amata*," he said, very seriously. "You must know that I was never going to send you away. I cannot exist without you. I do not wish to. And we will have as many children as you like, who you can tether to yourself if you so wish." He leaned forward then, and slowly, with great deliberation, began to kiss each and every tear from her cheeks. "I only ask that this tether does not extend into our bed."

"Of course not," she whispered back, her own laughter catching in her throat. "Whatever do you take me for?"

High above them, the clouds were finally gone. The moon beamed down, making the gardens they found themselves in glow silvery and bright.

It was not warm, so neither one of them removed their clothing. But he pulled her over his lap and she worked between them until she could take him inside her, and then they moved there, whispering their vows to each other as the long, dark night faded away all around them.

Again and again, they consecrated this new union, this new, true wedding.

And when the morning dawned, it was cold, but it was spring.

Gianluca and his wife rose together and breathed in the new day, the new season. They clasped their hands together, hung on tight, and walked back toward the palace. Because flowers weren't the only thing that could come back to life after a long, cold winter.

He looked down at this woman who he had given no reason to love him, no reason to trust him ever again, who had nonetheless placed not only her life, but the life of their child in his hands.

And Gianluca knew that no matter what came next, he would do his best to make certain that no winter was overtly long, that no deep freeze could not be melted, and that every summer was bright and bold enough to last them all the way through until the next one.

Because his Helene deserved to bloom.

CHAPTER TWELVE

THE FIRST THING Gianluca did was set about beginning the process of repairing his relationship with Elettra.

Their initial conversation, consisting mostly of apologies, was not long. And moving forward was not easy. It was, he discovered, less the repairing of a relationship and more the building of one. And it would have been only too easy to simply step back from this peace he was trying to weave.

But he didn't.

Because each time that happened, Helene was there, whispering to him of *tapestries.*

She was compassionate, understanding, and on the occasions—the very rare occasions, in his opinion—when he was entirely too bullheaded to listen to reason, prepared to fight him *for* him.

To shock him into listening to reason, if necessary.

He could not say he enjoyed it while it was happening, but in time, he came to depend upon her quiet reason and her willingness to challenge him when no one else would. Her acceptance of the intense emotions he tried to hide away, afraid who he would become if he was anything less than perfect.

And so, in time, he learned how to feel what he felt and express it, perhaps not immediately, but always appropriately.

Gianluca returned this favor by encouraging his reserved, masked paragon to show the world more of the Helene he knew, so that as the years passed, she became as well known for her laughter and her sense of humor as her good works and great dignity.

When it came to their children, she took him at his word that night. Their daughter was born with a head of dark hair, and his mother's gold-tipped eyes. And she was followed soon after by six more perfect, gold-eyed babies in rapid succession, because, as Helene would say to anyone who asked, she and Gianluca had always wished for siblings.

Their children, she laughed, would no doubt choose the opposite, after all the noise and joy and laughter.

But what they would not do was grow up cold

and afraid, forced to be spotless, and uncertain whether or not they were loved beyond reason.

Her much-adored cousin Faith became the sister Gianluca never had. She married for love as Helene had said she would, but Helene—apparently not trusting that love would show up in time—arranged the meeting. She made sure that her cousin got to know none other than Lady Lorenza's aristocratic, anthropologist, academic son.

"I think they might have some things to talk about," she said.

And she was right.

Their eventual marriage had many knock-on effects, one of which was the fact that Lorenza and Elettra were finally forced to truly get to know each other, instead of merely reading about each other in the papers.

Not that either one admitted they did such a thing.

And having witnessed the kind of magic Helene was capable of kicking up in her wake, wherever she went, Gianluca was not the least bit surprised that soon enough, the women his father had tried so hard to destroy became the very best of friends.

Years later, when Elettra told him that she had been approached to write a tell-all memoir, but would never so disrespect the throne, he told her to go right ahead.

"My darling son, I cannot promise I will keep anyone safe," Elettra told him.

She still lived in the dower house, because she was forever a champion and she still loved to ride, and could not give up her access to the stables.

But he had long since gotten rid of the guard at her door.

"No one kept you safe," he said, and then, recalling a little boy on his mother's lap, he smiled. "You tell your story as you wish, Mammina."

When her book came out, exposing the truth about his father for all the world to see, Gianluca was first in line to buy it. And he made certain that it was captured on every camera in Fiammetta, so there could be no doubt where his sympathies lay.

For no longer did he feel he had to prove himself to his people. He did that every day. The proof was in his policies.

He made no promises whatsoever to be perfect, and he knew he wasn't. He could only rule as best he could, always keeping his people in the forefront of his mind, not his own concerns.

And this was what he told his daughter, the Crown Princess Angelica. He did not speak to her of compartments and partitions. He did not try to leverage her affection. She was a levelheaded girl, more like her mother than like him, and he told her things his father would never have said to him.

"You must reign with your heart," he told her. "But rule with your head."

"And what if those two things do not align?" Angelica asked, because, at sixteen she was a smart, serious girl who knew her own destiny, but had a mischievous streak that made him far happier than it should.

And her mother was only starting to come around to the idea that she might wish to go off and live her own life—or at least have a few years of school and horizon-building before getting down to her royal duties.

"But that is the point," he told this marvel of a girl that he and Helene had made together. "It is not your job to align them. It is to honor both in every decision you make."

That was what he strove to do.

And every night, he and the Queen would step into their rooms, and become…simply themselves. Gianluca and Helene, who loved each other and held each other, comforted each other and soothed each other's wounds.

Day after day, year after year.

They held hands in the backs of cars, no words necessary…on the occasions they did not use that backseat for other, hotter things. They danced at a great many formal events but they also danced when they were alone. She would tip her head back and her smile reminded him of summer in Provence, and she told him he was all the music she needed.

They laughed so much it hurt, they loved their children wildly, and every room in the whole of the palace sang with the force of all the things they were to each other.

"Like a fairy tale," he liked to tell her, his mouth at her ear.

"Because," his Helene said when they were both very old, still smiling at each other over sprigs of lavender and melodies only they could hear until they made their great-grandchildren groan, "happy ever after is just another way of saying...*us*."

* * * * *

Were you blown away by
Wedding Night in the King's Bed*?
Then don't miss out on these other
pulse-racing stories by Caitlin Crews!*

A Secret Heir to Secure His Throne
What Her Sicilian Husband Desires
The Desert King's Kidnapped Virgin
The Spaniard's Last-Minute Wife
A Billion-Dollar Heir for Christmas

Available now!